WINGING IT

WINGING IT

A TALE OF
TURNING THIRTY

ELIZABETH TIPPENS

RIVERHEAD BOOKS
NEW YORK

Riverhead Books
Published by The Berkley Publishing Group
200 Madison Avenue
New York, New York 10016

Book design by Stanley S. Drate/Folio Graphics Company, Inc.
Cover photo: Larry Bercow

First edition: May 1996

Library of Congress Cataloging-in-Publication Data

Tippens, Elizabeth.
    Winging it : a tale of turning thirty / Elizabeth Tippens. — 1st
ed.
      p.   cm.
   ISBN 1-57322-528-2
   1. Young women—New York (N.Y.)—Fiction.   I. Title.
PS3570.I59W56   1996
813'.54—dc20   95-25421
                                              CIP

Printed in the United States of America

10 9 8 7 6 5 4 3 2 1

To my David

Many, many thanks to the following people, all of whom helped me enormously in one way or another, at one time or another: Gail Greiner, for her generosity; Jennifer Rudolph Walsh, for her brightness and faith; Cindy Spiegel, for her insight and guidance.

Plus Virginia Barber, Steven Streeter, Adam Sexton, Rosalind Winter, Ellen Bialo, and Sandra Schwartz.

Many thanks also to my parents, Frederick Tippens and Dorothy Tippens—always in my heart. And to my brother, Frederick M. Tippens, and my sister, Sandra Boynton.

And especially to J. R. Humphries, for lessons in writing and life.

CONTENTS

PERFUME

The man asked the girl to go to the South of France with him.

"You're not married, are you?" she asked.

"Pretty much," he answered. "Does it make a difference?"

"Well," she hesitated.

She was surprised when he simply began to walk away without so much as a wave good-bye.

"Wait," she called after him. A man like this man did not enter her orbit every day. She couldn't just let him drift away, round the corner, never to be seen or heard from again.

"There are worse crimes, I suppose," she called.

He turned and smiled. His teeth looked expensive.

"I'm all yours," she said, extending her arms like the gesture of a singer at the end of a song.

She had never been abroad.

The girl had known the man for only two weeks when together they boarded a night flight from New York to Paris, France, and then flew down from Paris to the small airport of Nice.

———

The girl nearly lost the man inside the Paris airport. She pounded the escalator stairs in her flat, white tennis shoes, trying not to bash right into people the way the man did. She said, "Excuse me, excuse me," as she fought the mob. She said, "Excuse me, excuse me," as she looked straight ahead like a racehorse in blinders, struggling to keep the man's broad shoulders ever in sight. He was way ahead of her.

She was dizzy with the thought of losing him. He spoke the language. He knew the currency. He carried her passport. Her luggage hung by long straps from his enormous shoulders. If she lost the man, she herself would be lost and alone in a strange country. She then felt certain this would happen. It was fear so acute it made her feel as though she knew something more than it was possible to know, some kind of precognition. Her mouth went dry, her temples pounded, and she began to run and to elbow people out of her way to catch up with him.

He stood waiting for her at the terminal. A look of impatience hardened his face, but made him look no less handsome. Winded and relieved, the girl smiled and waited for the man to smile, too.

"You've got to try and keep up with me," he said.

She felt flattened by his words and didn't smile anymore.

With the plane in flight, over the engine's steady

growl, the man turned to the girl and said, nicely, "You wouldn't want to wait around the airport for the next plane south, now would you?"

She wouldn't answer him. She looked out the window at the sky of unvaried, endless blue. Cartoon blue. It was the kind of blue you never see in New York. There, if you catch a patch of it between tall buildings, you cannot linger, looking up. You'll be trampled, or run down by a bus.

"Can't we be friends again?" he asked.

"Let's not get carried away," she said in the smart, dry way she could affect. She could make herself sound savvy almost, kind of wry. She knew this was how the man thought of her, why he liked her even, and why he'd invited her along. He probably thought she'd be fun, too young to be filled with any complicated emotions. She was supposed to be a playful kind of girl, and no trouble at all.

He pulled her by her shoulder into his side. She let herself be pulled by him, and held, and comforted a little by the warmth of his body and the clean smell of him. The man took her hand and squeezed. His hand swelled with veins and muscles and looked swarthy like the hand of a pirate. It was not the hand of a businessman at all, she thought. His hand squeezed hers, gripping it tightly.

"Traveling companions at least?" he asked.

"What choice do I have? You've got my ticket home."

The man laughed and relaxed his grip on her hand, and she could tell he felt the situation had been sufficiently smoothed over.

❧

The girl had met the man one afternoon at Bloomingdale's. She was studying acting and working to support herself as one of those people who try to spray other people with perfume. She had sprayed the man as he walked by, sprayed him on impulse, without his permission. She had a feeling he'd laugh if she sprayed him, and when she sprayed him he did laugh.

He took her out to lunch the following day. They ate sushi at a Japanese place in midtown. They sat on mats in their sock feet, surrounded by Japanese businessmen. There was smoking and card playing in the back room. The girl wondered if geisha girls really existed, and if they were in the back room, too. The man ordered in Japanese, fearlessly. She sat eating *hiziki* (seaweed) with chopsticks from a blue and white porcelain bowl, wondering if she'd ever see the man again. She liked his black, curly hair. She liked the large size of his hands. She stared at him, admiring his deftness with the chopsticks. She longed to reach out and feel the buttery leather of his jacket. He walked with his hands in its pockets as he escorted her back to Bloomingdale's.

Something about the man made her think of him as capable. Certainly he was a city man, but he possessed a resourcefulness she felt would translate from city to country, from one culture to another. He seemed to her the kind of man you'd be glad to have along in an emergency, like if your boat washed ashore on some deserted island, he'd be the one to take command, to tell you what to do first, and to tell you to stay calm. It was her first year in New York City, but she often thought about survival in the wild.

He asked her for dinner the following night. She borrowed something beautiful to wear from another girl, Missy, who also sprayed perfume. Missy was a gifted shoplifter.

In the days that followed the man and the girl had dinner many times. Afterward, he'd drive her home to her apartment in Hell's Kitchen. He was the only person she'd met in New York who owned a car. When they got there they would stand just inside her doorway and kiss, small, soft, cool kisses. He knew right where to place his hands when he kissed her—on her face, her neck, but he never once came all the way inside her apartment.

When they landed in Nice they were told their luggage had been lost. The man rented a VW Golf convertible, red, and they drove to their hotel in Cannes without their bags.

"My stuff," said the girl.

"They'll find it," said the man.

"What if they don't?" she asked, frantic. He didn't understand, she thought. If she lost things she couldn't afford to replace them. If she lost things they were gone for good.

"If they don't find it, I'll buy you all new clothes," said the man, downshifting, changing gears with easy precision.

Somehow she did not feel relieved. She watched the wind blow his black hair completely flat.

"See this scar on my forehead?" he asked.

She noticed the faded line indented into his skin just as he said this. It was high, along the hairline.

"Yes," she answered loudly to be heard above the wind.

"Right here on this road is where I cracked my head open. I was drunk, going fast. That was twenty years ago," he said with a laugh. He shook his head. "I was crazy then, a lunatic."

The girl began to feel the buzz of a sleepless night.

The sky was cloudless as they entered the city of Cannes. The horizon looked painted like a movie backdrop done in one solid, vibrant blue. No distinguishable line separated the sky from the sea. She felt the horizon contained an almost unnatural amount of blue. Its blue went on for what looked to be miles. The possibility of mirage occurred to her. She began to feel strange. Perhaps it is the deprivation, she thought, not having seen much blue in a long time, and now to be given blue in such uncontained abundance. A sensory overload, she decided. She felt a little shaky and leaned on the man's arm as they walked from the car to their room at Grand-Hotel.

She flopped down onto the bed and the man flopped down next to her. He removed all of her clothes, and she noticed the way he did it, deftly, expertly, they seemed to come off easily. They made love immediately, which surprised her. It felt good and she wrapped her legs around him, but still, she'd thought it was going to happen differently. She'd thought it would be more romantic, after dinner maybe, or after a long walk down the beach during which they would hold hands and talk a lot. They showered and made love again. Those small kisses seemed so fragile now that he had kissed her mouth until her lips felt swollen. He held her face in his hands and something in the gesture made her want to cry. Fatigue, she thought. "I need sleep," she murmured.

When she woke up she saw that the man had been out shopping and had returned with a black two-piece bathing suit. It made her anxious that he had not slept at all. She worried that she would not be able to keep up with him.

"But of course you only need the bottoms," he said, holding up the suit.

"Of course," she said.

She wore the hotel's thick, white terry-cloth robe to cover herself. The man stopped at the desk and offered to buy the bathrobe from the hotel. In French he explained about the lost luggage. The manager seemed to be offering to let the girl have the bathrobe, but the man insisted on buying it, and paid the concierge in cash.

Outside the air was balmy and smelled sweet from the grass and the flowers on the hotel lawn.

The man paid for their admittance to a private beach called Club Plage du Sport. The girl watched as deeply tanned men and women in bikinis whacked the volleyball back and forth across the net. The man joined their game and the girl noticed how much bigger he was than the European men playing ball, how he stood out among them.

The girl walked to the edge of the water. The water

seemed to strike the sand with a delicate precision. There was a daintiness to it. The sea foam left lacy white ruffles all along the shore. Everything seemed in miniature, the cushioned lounge chairs, the red canvas umbrellas, the well-manicured beach itself—everything except the man.

He was covered with sweat and sand when he finished his game. He pulled the girl by her arm toward the water. She laughed and screamed and the two of them dove into the sea together.

When they came back to shore the man stretched out and fell asleep beside her. She thought of touching him but decided not to. She couldn't understand what prevented her from stroking his sleeping face, something though.

At a beach café, they drank small glasses of sweet, watery orange liquid without ice. As the girl savored its taste she noticed a woman with long dark hair sitting nearby. Something about the woman made her stare, and the girl became fascinated by the way the woman wore expensive snakeskin heels without stockings. She wore the shoes bare-legged to the beach with her silver one-piece bathing suit; she wore the snakeskin shoes casually, as though they were of no more worth than cheap rubber sandals. This was the kind of easy glamour the girl was after, this kind of chic. The girl found herself admiring this woman, and wishing to put herself in those shoes.

In the late afternoon the man took the girl shopping for new clothes. The saleswomen were slim and elegant. They all had the same paper-white skin. Their lips, cheeks, and eyes had been brought to life with cool, translucent pinks and purples. Their fingernails were long and looked like bright, hard, shiny bits of plastic. Some of them wore large black velvet bows in their slicked-back hair. The girl thought of the young women who worked at Bloomingdale's. She thought of the runs in their panty hose and the chips in their nail polish, of the effort it took for them all to bring the store's version of reality to life on a day-to-day basis.

Each new thing she tried on made her want to dance. A yellow silk skirt made her twirl around in circles inside a small boutique. This seemed to delight the man who cheerfully paid the price of anything she chose. It was fun not caring how much things cost, and surprisingly easy.

Walking back to the hotel the girl stopped cold in front of a shoe store window.

"Look," she cried.

He took her inside and bought her the snakeskin shoes.

At night the man slept very soundly. He looked as many miles away from her as she felt herself to be from her small apartment in New York, and farther still from her small town in Virginia. But his body emitted so much heat, she needed no covers to stay comfortable. She had always been too cold at night. The blood in her feet and hands didn't circulate well, and even through the hot summer nights of New York her feet turned to ice. At home she kept several pairs of socks inside her pillowcase. Now she only had to press her feet against the man's feet to warm them. The man did not mind. He got too hot at night, almost feverish, he told her, and felt cooled by her freezing feet.

In the morning she woke to find they'd slept far apart from one another in the bed. They drank their dark coffee and ate their buttered croissants on the balcony. The girl knew she'd dreamed about the new snakeskin shoes, but looking out to sea she couldn't remember anything of what happened in the dream.

The man spent each morning attending to some kind of business. He was a record producer and had come here for MIDEM, the international music market held in Cannes each year. One morning the girl got a manicure downstairs at the hotel's beauty salon. They painted the tips of her fingernails white. When it came time to pay, the girl asked the manicurist for help.

"How much money do I have?" she asked the woman.

"Chérie, " the woman answered her, "you could buy a house."

The girl suddenly felt lonely and wished Missy, the other girl who sprayed perfume at Bloomingdale's, were with her. Missy was an expert at interpreting dreams. Missy would love to have a French manicure, too. And the two of them would find so many things to laugh about.

Knowing nothing of the language, the girl felt closed off from the world around her. She lay on the beach, sunbathing alone. Time would float by until around noon when the man would join her on the beach. Then things would begin to snap back into focus again. Rejoicing at the sound of her own voice, she'd say, "Hello, hello, hello. I was almost beginning to miss you."

The man loved fine food and at night they ate beautiful meals at expensive restaurants. The luggage had not turned up, and everything she wore was new. They'd return from dinner, fall into bed half-drunk, and make love. The man's lovemaking lacked tenderness, but once the girl realized he would only go about it one way, like an athlete, she began to take it for what it was, to adapt, and to like it as he did. Afterward they'd fall asleep, but the girl's cold feet would always wake her. She'd search for socks inside her pillow before she'd remember where she was. She'd feel the man next to her and warm her feet against his skin.

One afternoon he took her shopping for perfume. He was too large for the small shop. Salesgirls in their white linen smocks gasped, afraid, each time he moved from one glass table to another. The man drew thin lipstick lines on the back of the girl's hand with testers.

"I suppose you're an expert on women's cosmetics, too," she said, teasing him.

"I know what looks good," said the man, taking his job seriously.

He brushed different colors of powdery blush onto her arm. The brush strokes tickled but she decided not to laugh.

"These ones are perfect for you," he said, selecting a few.

The girl admired a giant bottle of Chanel, and the man had the salesgirl pull it from the shelf. The shop owner wrapped their purchases carefully. The man sent the girl ahead to the next shop while he stayed behind and paid.

Back at the hotel the man showered and dressed for dinner. From the bed the girl watched him pulling up his trousers, their creases perfect. He buttoned his shirt. He kissed her quickly and left to go downstairs for a drink on the terrace. The girl bathed, and naked, she admired her suntan in the mirror. She liked the way her hair had changed color. It was filled with golden sparkles, streaked very blond from the sun. She wrapped herself in a bath towel and went out onto the balcony. She leaned over the railing and watched the man as he sat in a wicker chair down below, playing backgammon with another man who wore a white suit and a Panama hat.

She dressed in a sleeveless black dress and the snakeskin shoes. She remembered the perfume and decided to open the new bottle. She searched for the bag and finally found it in the closet on the man's side, there on the floor underneath his hanging clothes. She opened the bag and pulled her perfume bottle from it. In the bag she found another bottle of perfume. It was Joy. She took it from its pink tissue paper wrapping, turned it over in her hands, wrapped it back up in the tissue, and returned it to the bag. She put the bag back in the closet on the man's side where she found it, dabbed on the perfume that belonged to her, and headed downstairs to meet the man.

When they arrived back at the hotel from dinner the girl went straight to the bathroom closet for her nail polish remover. The manicure she'd gotten was beginning to chip and fade. The polish had lost its luster, and she had spent dinner feeling self-conscious about the unkempt state of her hands.

She sat down on the edge of the bed and rubbed

away the polish with cotton balls doused in acetate solution.

"Jesus, that stuff stinks," said the man, hanging up his shirt on his side of the closet.

The man threw open the balcony doors, letting in the sweet night air. He waved his arms around to shoo the odor out of the room.

"Christ, I hate that smell," he said, his facial muscles making a big show of how unpleasant he found it.

"Sorry," said the girl as she rose, taking the whole operation into the bathroom.

"Can't you do that on your own time?" he called after her.

In the bathroom she washed her hands of the stuff with soap and water.

"Okay, okay," she said quietly. She was finished anyhow.

In bed that night the man's body failed to warm her feet. She got up and went to the bureau to get a pair of socks. She began to search the drawers before she realized she didn't have any socks. She'd packed a pair of short white lacy ones, but they were somewhere else, lost like the rest of her clothes. She thought of borrowing a pair of socks from the man's side of the drawer, but decided against it and wrapped her feet up in a hotel blanket.

The next morning she lay on the beach until she

thought the man would be through with his business meetings. She decided to surprise him in the room, where he would be changing into his swimming suit. As she approached the door she heard the man's voice from within. He was speaking in English on the telephone.

"I'll take care of it when I get home," he said. "Miss you. Love you," he said. "Love to the kids, too."

A different kind of woman would intrude, and even though it wouldn't be rational or particularly wise, that kind of woman would make a small scene, thought the girl. And still another kind of woman would laugh and tease the man for being so bad, off on an illicit little trip with his mistress. But she was neither kind of woman and a numb feeling spread throughout her body.

She walked back outside where the sun seemed very bright. She'd been trying hard to forget that the man wasn't hers, that after the South of France it was very likely she'd never see him again. And children, she hadn't wanted to imagine children at all. She fell asleep on the beach and when she woke up she was startled to find herself there. Someone had pitched an umbrella close by and shade covered her body. She felt a chill across her back, a chill that penetrated below the surface of her skin and caused all of her muscles to tighten against it. She looked up to see the man, who was at the net, leaping and diving for the volleyball. As she watched him there she saw for the first time that he was not playing at the game at all. She saw in the screwed-up muscles of his face that he was dead set on winning, and that winning meant everything.

After the girl had dressed for dinner, she sat down on the edge of the bed and looked down at her suntanned legs. They had become as smooth and as dark as the legs of the woman in the snakeskin shoes. She looked at her feet. Just the right amount of toe cleavage showed in the snakeskin shoes of her own. She thought of the dark-haired woman sitting all alone in her high-heeled shoes and her high-cut silver bathing suit. She thought of the languorous way the woman smoked, sat, drank, and how she had slowly run her hand down the length of her bare leg, the way you would to check the seam of your stocking.

The man took the girl to a place called L'Oasis where they sat inside a glassed-in gallery surrounded by a flower garden. She watched the untanned laugh lines around his eyes. He looked a little older than he had before. His face in repose looked empty. He tried to take hold of her hand but she pulled away from him and scratched the sunburn on her neck. From behind her the girl overheard someone say, "Rich Americans will anchor their yachts in Cannes tonight and let off a show of firecrackers."

"Fireworks," said the man, but she wasn't paying

any attention to him now. She'd spotted the woman in the snakeskin shoes, sitting at the bar drinking a kir royale and arguing quietly with the maître d'. Suddenly the maître d' grabbed hold of the woman's arm and held it very firmly. The woman tried to jerk her arm away but he managed to pull her from her bar stool to escort her to the door. A small beaded purse bumped against her hip as she walked.

"That woman," said the girl to the man, "he threw her out, did you see?"

It had happened swiftly and had not caused a commotion.

"Sure," said the man, "this is a four-star restaurant, they don't want hookers in here."

He signaled the waiter to bring the check.

"We'll go to the fireworks then," he said, finally capturing her hand.

Out on the beach that night white rockets raced through the sky, exploding into rings and rings of red and blue sparkling light. They walked along the pier until the man stopped to look into one of those machines that you put a coin into and see things that are very far away.

"I can never focus these things," said the man, fooling with it. "I look and look and end up seeing nothing."

The girl sat down on the concrete bench and breathed deeply. The sea air suddenly seemed intoxicating. Perhaps it was the pink and purple flowers that bloomed all over the Riviera, but something made the atmosphere too sweet, cloudy with its fragrance. The air felt heavy and each time she filled her lungs with it, she imagined too much of the stuff was entering her body. Like perfume, even the expensive kind, enough of it would finally make you sick.

"I'm going to need my ticket home," she said to the man.

He stepped away from his viewing machine to face her. In the dark his eyes had no color at all, only a lifeless gleam.

"What do you mean?" he said with a laugh. "Why would you say a thing like that?"

"I just want to go home, that's all," she said, her voice unexpectedly firm.

"Look, kid," he said calmly. She could see he was gathering his wits. "You're being stupid, okay. This trip is almost over. I think I've more than shown you a very nice time. What's the point of acting out a big drama now?"

She could not think of anything smart to say. She only wanted to return to her life and her possessions, which, however shabby, were her own. She stood and walked away, back in the direction of the hotel.

"Well, you're being stupid," she heard him say. She thought she heard a coldness in his voice and a hint of a cruel kind of laughter.

She pulled her arms into her chest, suddenly afraid he'd come after her, afraid of having her flesh dug into by his large thumbs. She took off the snakeskin shoes, and barefoot, she hurried along the boulevard, past the hookers and the tourists and the things the street vendors had for sale. She eyed the merchandise, thinking only of her missing suitcase. It was somewhere, full of her lost belongings.

LIKEWISE

"What am I to you?" she asks him.

"You're you to me," he answers. His stride is long. She is nearly trotting to keep up.

"I'm me to you?"

"Yes, you're you to me."

"What place do I occupy in your life?" she asks.

"A place of high regard. I regard you very highly."

"And what do you regard me so highly as?"

"I don't catch your drift," he says, catching it.

Lenny makes Faith's arms feel weak. Not in a good way. Not in a swooning way. Weak in a weak way. She trots along, weak arms dangling listlessly at her sides, knowing well what a large mistake it is to pursue this particular line of questioning, and knowing also that it is too late to unpursue it, too.

"From your point of view," she asks, "what is the purpose of me in your life?"

"That's easy," he says, tossing his large arm around her shoulder, pulling her in close. "You provide the substance."

"What kind of substance?" she asks.

"The kind of substance I was too preoccupied to think about on the way up."

———

25

"Preoccupied with what?" she asks, realizing at once that she has been made to veer off course.

"Getting big," he says, laughing, putting an ironic spin on the words. He can afford a winning tone of self-mockery. He can afford a lot of things. "Now that I've arrived, I want a little substance." He squeezes her arm. Black sneakers give his walk a little bounce. Or maybe it's life, she thinks. Not everyone in black sneakers bounces like that.

"That's me," she says, "Miss Substance." Now she is quiet. She needs time to regroup, time to process this information, which she knows has been handed out as a tactic, a diversion. Who can object to being the substantive one? To being loved for your ideals? He is tricky. She remains on the lookout for tricks, which is all she can do lately. Lately, she has been imagining an outdoor tomato garden on the terrace, which wraps around Lenny's penthouse apartment. She sees herself gardening there, weeding, pruning, humming. It is too late, she sees. She has already got the whole thing landscaped perfectly in her mind.

"Kid," he says, "you've got substance big time. Also, I like your hair."

"Likewise," she says.

They have arrived at their destination, a small frame shop on upper Broadway, a cozy three steps below sidewalk level.

It is Saturday and the shop is busy. Young salespeople, art students in black, help the customers measure posters, prints, and photographs for framing. She has brought a van Gogh print, *van Gogh in Arles*. She loves the painting, the brush strokes full of movement, southern breezes blowing gently over purple fields, grain of some kind, wheat, and a farmer, toting bales. It reminds her of a place, of a trip they took, of him. The farmer is Lenny, broad-shouldered, big, capable, and strong. He is always calling himself a peasant at heart. "I'm actually a potato farmer," he likes to say. But he is a potato farmer who has arrived, and is tired of coming over to her place and looking at an unframed poster stuck to the wall with two bent thumbtacks.

Lenny unrolls the print with a flourish, a snap. "We'd like a frame for this," he tells an awkward-looking Chinese boy dressed in baggy black pants.

The boy measures while they wander around the store looking.

Faith watches Lenny study a line drawing, one of Picasso's artful squiggles. He is definitely someone who someone's mother would call unsuitable. Why does she love the damp, tanned skin on his neck? Why does she want to smell him, kiss him there? Why is he always so tan anyway? Why does she always have to find him so dashing in a raincoat, getting out of a cab? Why can't she develop an interest in someone else, someone younger, someone who doesn't view himself as an arriviste/potato farmer. Someone who loves only her.

"Hello," she says, joining him at the Picasso, amazed that he has spent so long in thoughtful examination. She slips her arm through his. "You like that?"

"Picasso once said, 'If you can't sell it, it ain't art,' " he tells her.

"What?" she says, snapping out of any daydream she may have been floating in. "Picasso never said that."

"Sure he did," he says.

"When?" she demands. "Under what circumstances?"

"Don't be naive," he says, "artists think more about money than bankers do."

"You don't know what you're talking about," she snaps. "Van Gogh would finish a painting and if he didn't like it, he'd just throw it out the window."

"Van Gogh was a nut," he says.

"Whoosh," she says, "he'd just hurl it right out the fucking window."

"Van Gogh was a kook. He cut off his own ear, for God's sake."

"You just don't understand a gesture like that."

"I understand it was a nutty thing to do."

"It was poetic. It was a poetic thing to do."

"Van Gogh didn't care about money because van Gogh was a fucking wing nut," he says loudly.

"Van Gogh was an artist," she fires back.

"So is the chef at my restaurant, but you don't see him cutting off his ear."

"The chef at your restaurant is not an artist."

"Have you seen what he can do with a tilefish?"

"I don't give a shit what he can do with a tilefish, a chef is not an artist."

"Well, if you haven't seen his tilefish . . ."

"Tilefish isn't art," she says, the pitch of her voice growing uncontrollably higher, the volume louder. "If you can eat it, it ain't art."

"Who says?"

"Van Gogh."

"Van Gogh was insane," he shouts, "certifiably insane."

"So, are we getting married or not?" she shouts back.

"What's that got to do with van Gogh?" he stammers, lowering his voice dramatically.

"It's a yes or no question, Lenny." Hands on hips, her arms are no longer weak. People are looking. The whole store is looking.

"This is hardly the place to discuss this, Faith."

"I think this is a fine place-to-discuss-this-Faith," she says.

"Well, I never said anything about getting married—I just got divorced, for fuck's sake."

"Untrue," she shouts, "you're the one who planted the marriage seed in my mind in the first place."

"And how did I do that?"

"You, not me, started saying things like: Our kids would have the most incredible calf muscles. Remember that one?"

"All I meant was that we both have big calves."

"You, not me," she goes on, "are the one who first put my first name together with your last name: Faith Finkelstein. Remember saying Faith Finkelstein? Not that I'd change my name anyway."

"At least I'm divorced," he shouts. "At least you're not skulking around with a married man anymore."

"I never skulked. I wasn't the married one."

The shop's owner, a petite Italian woman, approaches, a look of horror enlarging her already big eyes. "My store is too small to fight in," she says. "I am afraid I am going to have to ask you two to leave."

"Ask us to leave?" says Lenny, turning toward the woman. "You'd have to pay me to stay."

"He's right," Faith tells the woman. "He's been kicked out of way better places than this."

"You, too, ma'am," says the owner. "I am asking both of you to leave."

"Ma'am," says Faith. "Did you hear that, Lenny?

She called me ma'am. I'm only twenty-five. Do I look like a ma'am? This relationship is aging me beyond my years. People are calling me ma'am!"

"You are both hysterics," says the woman. "Get out."

Out on the sidewalk the sun shines brilliantly, and the tranquillity of the day seems strange. People amble by with their purchases, their dogs, their ice cream cones, their children.

"Did she mean we were *in* hysterics," asks Faith, "or that we *were* hysterics, as in some kind of clinical Freudian diagnosis?" She clutches her unframed print. She feels like crying. "I've been kicked out of a store," she says.

"Fuck her," says Lenny, gathering himself, then pulling Faith by the arm. "If she were a man, I would have popped her."

"There is a problem with this arrangement," says Faith, trailing behind once again, weak-armed once again.

"And what's that?"

"I don't always want to be the one with substance."

"Okay," he says, "we'll switch. You be the asshole, I'll be the high-minded one."

"There is another problem with this arrangement," she says, stopping now, standing still.

He stops, too.

"Yes or no?" she says.

"Yes or no what?" he says.

"You know."

"Know what?" he says, stalling.

Faith knows that as far as Lenny is concerned there is always a gray area, a nice shady respite where shapes shift and endless life configurations abound and nothing definitive need ever reside. She waits, hoping this once for something black or white.

"Good-bye," she says, turning, beginning to walk away, a now bent and wrinkled *van Gogh in Arles* tucked under her arm.

She reaches the light and wonders which way to go when he appears at her side, offering his arm.

FIREFLIES

Every so often my old boyfriend calls and asks me, would I like to go sit somewhere and have a glass of wine this Sunday, if I'm not going away for the weekend, that is.

This time I say, "I'm not going anywhere, but maybe it's not such a hot idea, you know?"

I tell him it would only lead to him trying to get back together with me, which would only lead to some big, ugly scene.

I say, "Remember the last big, ugly scene?"

The truth is that right now, hearing his voice, I don't want to remember the last big, ugly scene. I have to think hard to conjure it. More truth is that I would love it, to go sit somewhere on a Sunday, at one of those outdoor cafés that spill out onto the sidewalk on Broadway or Columbus Avenue. I could wear a skirt and flat sandals and my hair pinned up on top of my head. I would feel my skin glow from spending the day at the health club, swimming and lying around on the sundeck reading the *Times Magazine* section and the Book Review. At the health club I wouldn't even care that nobody ever speaks to me, or that nobody ever speaks to anybody. I'd know that later on I would be sitting, having a glass of wine, having a conversation, and I would feel pretty.

The white wine would be very cool. It would sparkle in the glass in the late-afternoon sun. I would look around me. The men in linen trousers and no socks would look chic, and I'd be glad that I live in New York City where the promise of a little glamour still exists. It would be nice to see my old boyfriend. He'd be wearing jeans and black sneakers and a summer sweater. The familiar shape of his very broad shoulders would make me feel comforted in a way I can never put my finger on. He would have ridden his bike and it would be chained to a signpost nearby. He is almost twice my age, and probably too old for me, but he would seem young because he would have been playing volleyball all weekend. It would be nice to see him, because, well, he would look good, and after all, he does have some lovely qualities. He knows a trick or two that a younger man has yet to learn. He would know what wine to order. It would sit in a wine bucket by his side and he would wrap the bottle in a towel and pour when he saw that my glass was running low.

I remember falling for my old boyfriend. I got a kick out of the brash new language he spoke, the very hippest kind of lawyerese. I admired his New Yorkness, his energetic combination of optimism and savvy, and a certain unabashedness. Once he followed me into my bank, snuck up behind me, and dug his big thumbs into my ribs. Through the very quiet bank air his very loud voice echoed, "Boo." I jumped, then screamed. Everybody stared. All at once I could be shocked and inspired by him, thrilled. He was spontaneous, fun, and at times only one step away from barbarism. He had been known to climb on top of city mailboxes, and standing tall, bellow for all he was worth. If I went with him for a drink on Sunday, he would be temporarily tame. From up his sleeve he would pull his best, most polished behavior.

Over the telephone, he asks, how was my birthday?

He is probably hoping that I'll remember last year when he threw me a big party. It was a spectacular affair, with balloons and a cake, but impersonal somehow, catered, and with my old boyfriend holed up in the bedroom watching basketball on T.V. He emerged every once in a while and refilled a few wineglasses and checked on the ice supply. He smiled at my guests. He shook a few hands and returned to the bedroom. I felt like a teenage girl on her birthday. Sweet sixteen. I think my friends felt sorry for me. They stayed very late and helped me clean up while we laughed and gossiped and recounted the events of the evening together.

My old boyfriend had long since fallen asleep on top of the bed in all of his clothes, the television blaring its late-night infomercials. I sat down on the edge of the bed and watched an elfin weight-loss guru hug a three-hundred-and-fifty-pound woman. "You matter to me," he told her. "Now matter to *you*."

"You mean, how was my birthday this year?" I ask my old boyfriend.

"This year," he says.

"This year? Oh, big. Major!"

He didn't call me, he tells me, because he was mad; I didn't call him on his birthday, which is, after all, a significant event in a person's life, especially when the person is turning fifty. Right?

"Right," I say.

This year my own birthday passed, without, as they say, occasion. I turned twenty-seven. I would have done something with my very best friend, Missy, but Missy had to leave the day before for a weekend seminar called "You're Not What I Expected: Dreams of the Opposite Sex," at the C. G. Jung Foundation. So I spent the day sunbathing at the health club. I bought myself an Oreo cheesecake at a gourmet food store. My parents left a singing message on my machine. My other best friend, Kenneth, called from somewhere in the state of Pennsylvania, where he is playing The Beanstalk in *Jack and the Beanstalk*, to tell tales of summerstock, a hell on earth. "An entire flock of geese attacked me," he said. "They were honking and flapping all over. I feared for my outfit, not to mention my life."

This year my birthday fell on a Sunday. I don't like Sundays, Sunday afternoons that is. On Sunday mornings I've taken to going to Quaker Meeting for Worship, at the Meeting House on the campus of Columbia University. I hadn't been since high school, but I started going again to give my Sunday mornings purpose. This way I don't lie in bed wondering if I should move or not.

Courtney Foley from my Quaker high school in Virginia has also moved to New York, also lives on the Upper West Side, and goes to the same Meeting for Worship. If I happen to look at her the whole thing degenerates into an hour-long memory of high school. Then I think Courtney Foley is glaring at me, sending me hate vibes because I played Mabel in *The Pirates of Penzance* while she sulked in the chorus. It is probably her memory that I was popular, which in a school of only two hundred students is not such a major feat. Occasionally in Quaker Meeting someone will be moved to stand and speak out in the silence. People say things about God or nature. I want to stand up and yell at Courtney Foley, *"There is no more popular anymore."*

"So, working hard?" my old boyfriend asks.

"I'm in transition," I say.

I'm a vegetarian, but two years ago I bit down hard into one of those huge, juicy hamburgers with layers of buns and lots of sauce and pickles and shredded lettuce, and I got my first commercial. At the moment all I seem to be getting are radio voice-overs for banks on Long Island and theme parks in New Jersey. Phyllis, my agent, says that my type is changing; I'm going from "Suzy College" to "Young Mom Driving the Kiddies to the Little League." I'm working on a new demo tape. The new tape will scream, I'm here, I'm still here, vroom, vroom, I'm driving those kids to the Little League.

At night I get these little attacks of panic. My arms get numb, then my chest gets tight and I'm sure I'm not breathing anymore. I can't figure out what I am thinking when this happens. Maybe every pessimistic statistic ever printed about modern love has seeped into my unconscious. Maybe it's one New Jersey theme park too many. Maybe it's negotiating the daily obstacle course of New York, keeping sharp the wits, staying loose, the constant state of improvisation.

At night I try to think of pleasant things. I used to lie in the dark and decorate my imaginary country house, but for a while now it has been finished. To continue would mean to redecorate, or, worse, to *over-*

decorate, and it is just exactly the way I want it. I can't help it, I love all that Laura Ashley stuff. (Oh, the tiny floral print!)

It's fireflies I think of now as I try to fall asleep at night. So I see them darting around in the dark of some backyard, lighting up all over, one here, one there. Quite recently I began to imagine the fireflies lighting up on the lawn of my country house. I build myself an imaginary porch, and now when I am watching them light up, I am sitting on the porch. I am aware of a man's presence. The man is not like my old boyfriend with his five grown children from a previous marriage, his too recent divorce, his bathroom cabinet filled with another girl's things, his strange inability to remember the names of my cats. This new man is young like me, and hopeful. He is standing up behind me and he rests a reassuring hand on my shoulder. Still looking ahead, I take his hand and squeeze. I am watching a child of mine dashing around the yard, scooping a rinsed-out mayonnaise jar through the twilight air, catching fireflies the way I used to.

~

I want badly to say yes to this proposition of a drink on Sunday. You can't go to those little places alone. People will stare. Or worse, someone out of the question will try and talk to you. I want to go. It's just one drink. Besides, I haven't been out, haven't met anybody in the longest time.

There was this one man with neat-looking, longish hair in the checkout line at the Food Emporium. I guess you could say we almost met. He smiled and said, "It looks like your cat eats better than you do."

"Cats," I said, stacking up the little cans, "I have two of them."

Then he asked if I thought my Chock Full o' Nuts was the best brand of coffee.

I said, yes, of the canned coffee, I thought it was the best.

Then he asked if I thought my Lorna Doones were the best brand of cookies.

I said, yes, of the store-bought variety, I thought they were the best. "It's hard to go wrong when a cookie has this much fat," I said.

Then he said he hoped I was going to eat more than just Lorna Doones.

I said, "I have this cold, so the whole eating thing is really unfocused." I heard this sentence come out of my mouth. In my head I thought, what?

It was Friday night at ten o'clock and he was buying root beer and breadsticks and one single roll of toilet paper. I imagined he was going home to his apartment to watch a movie on his VCR. That's where I was going too, with my cat food and my coffee and my Lorna Doones and my vitamin C. He left saying, "Have a good weekend."

In two separate conversations I wailed to both Kenneth and Missy on the phone. What was I supposed to do? What was he supposed to do? What is anybody supposed to do? Maybe if I hadn't had this stupid cold fogging up my brain I would have been more on top of the situation. Who gets a cold in summer anyway?

"So, how about that drink on Sunday?" my old boyfriend says. "I promise not to hold your hand."

I remember such promises. And now I remember that big, ugly scene I don't wish to repeat took place in a restaurant. Doesn't it always?

We bumped into each other on the street the day after Thanksgiving. I was squishing along in wet running shoes, under a fluorescent safety-orange umbrella, when I heard a low, gravelly voice saying, "Hey you."

I whipped around, ready to tell whoever it was to just please drop dead, when I saw it was him.

"Oh, Jesus, I thought you were some masher," I said.

"Aren't I a masher?" He was smiling.

"Absolutely," I said, "I just thought you were a masher I didn't know."

We both laughed. My heart was pounding inside my chest, quite against my will. He was wearing his green jacket with the rip in the sleeve. I wanted to tell him to get the sleeve of his jacket sewn up, or to get a new jacket. It was wet out, pouring rain, but he looked dry and possibly warm. I had to resist an impulse to abandon my own umbrella and join him under his.

So, the next afternoon he called. Of course.

At first I said no to going out for dinner just to talk.

"But we ran into each other in the middle of Manhattan," he said. "We have karma together."

"Bad karma," I said. "Besides, karma is from the sixties."

"Yes," he said, "but so am I."

"True," I said and laughed. He could do that to me sometimes, make me laugh utterly against my will. I had to acknowledge the existence of some kind of force, bad or good or outdated, that caused us to bump into each other and to dwell on each other and to become nostalgic.

We got together at a restaurant in the Village that only serves fish. He tried to hold my hand, but I reached for my water glass and avoided his grasp. He looked tired and his curly black hair looked wiry, which is how it got when he had a cold or was extremely tired. It's probably a mistake to go out with your old boyfriend around the holidays, I thought. But when it comes to my old boyfriend, what I know and what I do cannot always be reconciled.

"I'm frustrated," he said at the restaurant, "I don't know what more I can say to convince you to give this another try." He shook his head. "My sales pitch is running out of steam."

"Quit trying to sell me. It's over," I said.

"God damn it," he shouted. His heavy fist came down hard on the wooden table. Frightened silverware jumped. My hands flew to cover my own gaping mouth, as if that would quiet things.

He reached across the table and pried my hands from my mouth. He held my palms to his face, and tears filled his eyes. The waiters were staring.

"Maybe you just don't love me anymore," he said.

This I couldn't answer. I thought, strangely I do, but I love you because I used to love you, and not because I love you now. An entire family at a nearby table were trying not to look. Their five-year-old boy was drumming on the table with his fork and knife, saying, "Mommy, Daddy, the world is spinning, the world is spinning."

And I felt it, with my old boyfriend's tears on my hands, I felt the world spinning. Our breaking apart had already been set in motion.

Our silence on the telephone makes me grit my teeth, tear at the skin around my fingernail. Now he asks me one last time.

"How about it? How would you like to go sit somewhere and have a glass of wine this Sunday?"

"I just don't think so," I say. "But thanks for calling."

"Are you seeing anybody? I just want to know."

"Yes," I tell him, "I am."

This is only a half lie since just last week I ran into somebody from my hometown and am definitely considering kissing him. At least.

"Uh-huh, I see," says my old boyfriend. "I see."

We hang up. I know him. He is persistent, part of what I like about him, and he will call again. He will force me to say what I already said without words, that time before when he managed to get hold of my hands. He is not the one.

I sit on my bed watching my cats, who are sitting in the window watching the little brown birds of summer land on the fire escape. I pick up the little cat, the one that likes to be picked up. I can't go for a drink on Sunday because if I do, I may never, ever get to my fireflies.

ORNI-
THOLOGY

I have been waiting years for Lenny's hair to turn gray. But will it? No. At the age of fifty-one not one boyishly curly hair on his head will whiten.

"How come?" I ask, pulling one of the curls out long and watching as it springs back into position.

"State of mind," he says.

I am absolutely sure he is right and the thought of all that willpower galvanizing itself to stave off the aging process makes my limbs feel heavy.

"Really, it's a bit much by now," I say.

"Now don't turn mean," he says, stroking my hair meditatively. "We've had such a lovely afternoon."

Lenny lives up high in a penthouse apartment on the Upper West Side of Manhattan. There are windows everywhere and outside the day has turned into late afternoon. The sun, which streaked across the floor and the bed and our bodies, is now gone away.

"I've got to go," I say, as though saying it will somehow bring me one step closer to making it happen.

"Stay awhile," Lenny says. "I've got hilarious people coming by for a drink. You'll get a kick out of them, I promise."

Lenny's friends bore me, except for the famous ones, and they make me jealous, which makes it impossible to tell whether they bore me or not. Trying to sort it all out causes confusion, which makes me withdraw, and become boring myself. Besides, today is my boyfriend Sandy's birthday. He is turning twenty-eight.

"Can't," I say, "it's Sandy's birthday. I'm cooking him dinner."

"You never cooked for me," he says, pouting.

"There are a lot of things I didn't do for you," I say. "Besides, Sandy is not like your gourmet self. He does not hover over me and criticize."

"I never criticized," he says, "I gave helpful suggestions."

"You hovered and you criticized," I say.

"Okay, so I hovered a little," he says. "What are you cooking?"

"Sea scallops and sautéed snow peas," I say.

"I taught you that," he says. "How dare you cook him *my* scallops and snow peas."

"You taught me everything I know," I say, patting his hand. "How can I even make a sandwich without using some part of the vast knowledge you imparted to me."

"You know, Faith, sarcasm is not really a very attractive quality," he says, draping his large body on top of mine.

"You're going to have to live with it, Mom," I say.

We kiss and my legs automatically wrap themselves around his back.

"I don't have time for this," I say.

He kisses me again and I feel his hardness against my stomach.

"I'm not kidding about this," I say, unwrapping my legs.

He pushes himself inside me and begins to move, slowly.

I love the clean way he smells; even his sweat smells clean.

"Enough," I say, because my body wants to move against his. "I don't have time."

"Jesus," he says, pulling out and rolling onto his back. "Go then. Get the hell out. I've got people coming anyway."

I get up and look around the floor for my underwear. Surveying his bachelor's bedroom, there seems to be no logic to the way my clothing has been discarded—a sock here, another clear across the room on the windowsill.

"What does this guy do again?" Lenny says, trying now to get a fix on Sandy.

Lenny knows perfectly well what Sandy does and

does not do. Lenny has made it his business to acquaint himself with Sandy's bio. He is relieved and made secure by what Sandy isn't, but the rest of it he finds maddeningly incomprehensible, the rest of it being what Sandy is.

"The Peace Corps and then the army?" Lenny asks.

"No," I say, "the other way around."

"And he's a graduate student studying what?"

"Ornithology."

"Which is what?" he asks, snapping his fingers, annoyed by his own lack of knowledge.

"Birds and anything about birds," I say.

"Yes, and what exactly is the appeal of this for you? What do you possibly do together?"

"We go to museums. I bet you never knew I liked that kind of thing. Well, I do. We go to the Museum of Natural History where there are plenty of stuffed penguins. Yes, *plenty* of stuffed penguins," I say, snapping my bra shut in front.

"You know what your problem is?" he says, sinking back into his goose-down pillows.

"No, but you do, right?" I say.

"You've forgotten what kind of girl you are."

"And what kind of girl is that?"

"You're a girl who likes nice things. You're a girl who likes good shoes and expensive restaurants."

"Yeah, well, I also like a man who is not the whore-master of the Upper West Side."

Lenny's face softens and he can't stop himself from smiling. He is a person who loves being characterized, no matter how unflattering the description.

"Don't you know a woman can forgive a man anything as long as he's rich," Lenny says, grinning now.

I look around the room, desperate for my jeans and sneakers.

"If the ornithology student is such a rich experience for you, what are you doing here with me?"

"Curiosity," I say, pulling on my jeans. "Sometimes I just like to come by to see if maybe your whole personality hasn't changed."

I sit down on the edge of the bed to tie the laces of my beat-up sneakers while Lenny goes into the bathroom for a quick shower. I look down at the hole in the toe of my shoe and I try not to think about Paris where the shoes do not get any more beguiling. In Paris the shoes dazzled. In Paris the shoes seduced. They sang songs, those Paris shoes, enticing tunes with promising upbeat lyrics. "Just direct your feet to the sunny side of the street," they sang. Lenny heard the way shoes sang to me. He heard their devilish little version of "Puttin' on the Ritz." He heard their two-part harmonies. "Kid, if you can carry it out of here, it's yours," he said. And I left the store with boxes of flats and pumps and boots

piled high against my chest, feeling like the winner of a
TV contest I'd seen as a child. That lucky winner was
set free to tear around a Toys "R" Us with a shopping
cart, and told she could keep whatever she could rip
from the shelves in ten minutes flat. Barbie, Ken, Skip-
per, Scooter, Barbie wardrobe, Barbie Dream Car, Barbie Dream House, Barbie World, Barbie Universe . . .
They let her keep it all.

A shockingly loud buzzer sounds in every room of
the apartment.

"The people," Lenny says, emerging from the bathroom, "they're here."

"Oh, Jesus," I say. "I can't do this anymore. It's
too much chaos for me. I've got to get to a grocery
store."

He sits down next to me on the bed and wraps his
big arms around me.

"One drink," he says. "One drink with a famous
heavy metal star. You'll laugh, I swear."

"No," I say firmly, "I've got to get to a grocery
store."

Out in the living room Lenny and I clink wineglasses
with a man and a woman with the same teased-up
hairdo and identical snakeskin cowboy boots. They are

both all height and bony angles, fascinatingly thin. His left ear is dotted in a semicircle with tiny gold earrings, and I recall reading that for reasons of personal superstition he pierces his left ear each time he crosses the equator.

"We're getting married," the heavy metal star says.

Lenny discovered him in a club in Atlanta during a snowstorm and has produced his last three albums. Now he's rich too, and has a ranch in Montana where he hunts deer and writes anti-gun control articles that actually see the light of publication in the pages of more than one glossy men's magazine.

"Do you hunt, too?" I ask the girl. They met two weeks ago in a radio station in Cleveland where she teaches aerobics to the staff and does a daily weather report.

"In a way," she says and laughs. She is beautiful really, with blue eyes and blond hair, a soft-looking girl even with the hard makeup and the spiky hair. They squeeze each other. They are in the kind of love that excludes the rest of this ordinary world, and you don't want to look while they kiss each other deeply with their tongues, but neither can you turn away.

"There is a dead spot in this room unless I turn on the radio," Lenny says. "Can't you people feel a dead spot?"

He crosses the room to turn on a jazz station, and

for a moment I imagine him slipping into that dead spot he's always talking about, and being lost forever, like one of those pilots who flies into the Bermuda Triangle and is never heard from again.

But the dead spot does not disturb the heavy metal star and his girlfriend, who continue their luxurious discovery of how one another should be kissed. I stand and stare, wondering why I can't just leave this place. I have Sandy now and I have important relationship business in my life, like Sandy's birthday dinner to prepare. Sandy came into my life and rescued me from this man whose bathroom cabinet would forever contain hair spray and nail polish that did not belong to me. I have Sandy now, a homey kind of man, the kind of man who enjoys taking out the garbage, the kind who knows his way around a hardware store and fixes broken toilets and erects new bookshelves, the kind of man who likes to nest. I have Sandy now who loves only me.

"I've got to get to the grocery store," I say.

"Faith was recently in an Off-Broadway play," Lenny says, beaming at me and squeezing me around the shoulder tightly.

"Lenny, please," I say, embarrassed. "They don't care." Lenny always tries to build up my résumé, to make the most of my achievements. But I have only the minimum amount of accomplishments you need in this city to have something to say for yourself at a cocktail party, no more.

"Hey," Lenny asks the heavy metal star, "did Ozzy Osbourne really bite the head off of a live bat in concert?"

"Gross," says the girl, making a face.

Lenny looks anxious. He promised me entertainment and now he looks concerned that the lovers are likely only to deliver to one another.

"Yeah, man, he did it," says the heavy metal star, still gazing into the eyes of his beloved.

"I heard that bats have become an endangered species," I say.

Everyone is quiet, and in this moment when we are all surely baffled to find ourselves in one another's company, Lenny, our host, fills our glasses with more red wine.

Outside the sky darkens quickly now. Lights from downtown buildings begin to twinkle and to wink.

To Sandy everything has something to do with love. He knows all about birds and their mating habits for instance, and when he sees birds, which is all of the time, he always seems to see them flying together in pairs. Love forms the basis of his worldview and many of his scientific theories. We argue about this and I point out that he is studying to be a scientist after all. What would Darwin say? But Sandy continues to find evidence to support his theories. He points to pictures of birds in bird books, birds who mate for life when they could propagate the species just as well by mating only for a season. "There must be a reason for it," I say. "There is," he tells me. "They're in love."

I spotted Sandy at the 24 hour Food Emporium near my apartment. I shopped late at night and he was working his way through school, stocking the shelves with fresh milk and yogurt. He was a mirage, an incongruous, puzzling vision there in aisle one.

"Hey, don't I know you from somewhere?" he said.

He is from the same small town in Virginia as I am and is perhaps the person I least expected to run into at the Food Emporium. I remembered him being shorter than me in seventh grade and walking to school with his viola, ready to use its sturdy black case as a weapon against anyone who made an unsolicited remark. I knew he had always been at least a little in love with me.

Now of course he was much taller, and without his viola. He had dark hair and deep blue eyes and velvety black eyebrows. He was handsome now, and armed with the kind of tip-your-hat, how-do-you-do-ma'am style of a Southern gentleman. Graciousness it's called; there is no other word for it. I felt unexpectedly comforted by a set of manners I understood the meaning of. Attracted, too. His mouth, which had been a little buck-toothed and goofy as a child, now looked full of erotic promise, kissable. And he could imitate a pigeon, the way it cooed and fluttered. Pigeons, he told me, were part of the dove family. A pigeon, he said, was really a dove.

I wondered if I could make him love me, hopelessly, the way I loved Lenny. I know. But I couldn't help it.

I have showered the scent of Lenny from my skin and brushed my teeth to get rid of the smell of red wine. Sandy comes up behind me to the stove where I am cooking, and presses his body up against mine. It's not possible, I think, to go on like this, is it?

"It's unbelievable," Sandy says into my neck, "but a pair of red-tailed hawks are nesting right up on 112th Street. I mean, what a birthday."

"The 'birders' must be thrilled," I say. "Birders" are what bird-watchers call themselves.

"We're unrelentingly thrilled," he says, squeezing me. "My life list will sure see some hot action tonight." A life list is a leather-bound journal in which birders record all of their most important sightings under headings like date, location, habitat, remarks, and though

Sandy has been a birder since he was a little boy, it is only since finding me at the 24-hour Food Emporium that he has actually begun his life list. "First I had to get a life," he told me.

He kisses my neck. "You are my bird-watching inspiration," he says.

I believe there is poetry hidden in that life list book, Sandy's secret poetry, scribbled indecipherably small between the entries, in the margins, in the back where it says "notes." The poetry would be about birds of course—hawks and eagles, and possibly me, perhaps being compared to a bird of some kind.

"Where do you think Venus came from?" he asks me.

"I don't know, a giant scallop," I say, trying to free myself from his grasp.

"See!" he says into my ear. This is part of Sandy's ongoing campaign to convince me that all the world and nature encourage love. He finds fruits, vegetables, and now seafood incredibly sexy.

He squeezes me tighter.

"Sandy," I say sharply, "if you don't get out of my way I'm going to burn these. This is twenty-two dollars' worth of sea scallops and I really don't want to burn them."

"Okay, okay," he says, backing out of the tiny kitchen area.

I arrange the scallops and snow peas on the plates and sprinkle them with parsley, quickly, and with some wrist action the way I've seen Lenny sprinkle parsley. The dish looks pretty and I feel encouraged. I can be this way, I think, a home person, someone who cooks for someone like Sandy.

I set the plates down on the place mats and Sandy lights the candles.

"They're burned," I say.

"No they're not," says Sandy, chewing.

"Well, not burned then, but overcooked," I say.

"They're delicious," he says.

"They're tough," I say. "They're tough and I've ruined your birthday dinner."

"Well, I'm eating them," he says, spearing a couple onto his fork. "I'm-gobbling-them-up-yum-yum."

"Really?" I ask, allowing myself to be reassured.

"Really," he tells me, "I could eat nothing but these sea scallops for the rest of my life."

Later on I say, "I'm so tired."

"I understand." Sandy always understands.

I touch his face. I never think to touch Lenny's face. I just don't.

I wake suddenly from a dream and am surprised to

find Sandy lying there next to me. In the dream I had unplugged my phone, answering machine and all, but Lenny had somehow gotten through. His voice came onto my machine, filling the room with its gravelly tones, low and intimate. It is a voice that sounds worn out from the ferocious making of deals, a voice that sounds ashamed of things and is finally ready to be nice.

Of course I did not mean to start up with Lenny again, and just maybe I would not have, if it had not been for the day I saw him crossing Broadway at around Seventy-first Street. I had nearly forgotten that walk of his with the little spring in its step, light for a man so muscle-bound and large. It surely knows some powerful secret that keeps it bouncing along. It is the gait of an optimist, and I must be near it to ape it or I forget how it goes. There on the street he spied me, too. "It's you," he said, no more than that, and my own unsteady footing was lost.

Sandy turns onto his side and even in the darkness I can see where the gray hairs have started to come in. I worry that I am somehow the cause of this premature aging. Sandy wants to get married as soon as he graduates, but he should not be here, I think. He dreams of large free birds, and I think he should probably go out West where they say the American eagle is making a comeback. A rare victory, they're calling it.

Sandy opens his eyes, stares blankly, sleepily, and shuts them again.

It is selfishness to keep him here in the city when they are going to need someone like Sandy to count eagles in Colorado.

"What's the matter?" he says.

"Can't sleep," I say.

He wraps both arms around me from behind and we lie, knees bent, like spoons in a drawer. Sandy always manages to find the most comfortable positions for our bodies to curl into.

"Here's a story," he says. He tells me little stories when I can't sleep at night.

"Before I met up with you," he begins, "my plastic army men were at war with my plastic dinosaurs. There were battles raging everywhere. In my closet, under my bed. Sometimes they brought the war right out in the open and fought all over the bookshelves."

"A terrible story," I say, closing my eyes.

"Oh, it gets worse. Before I met up with you I was having conversations with myself."

"Like what?" I feel sleepy now, lulled by Sandy's voice.

"Hey, pal, can we get away with wearing these socks another day, or should we get a cleaner pair out of the dirty laundry bag. What do you say, Big Guy?"

"You're delirious," I say.

"I know," he says, "can you sleep now?"

I can feel Sandy's long eyelashes against my cheek.

"One more short one," he says sleepily. "Before I found you again I was like a piece of Swiss cheese."

"How so?" I murmur.

"Shot full of holes."

Since Sandy moved out of his Columbia University housing and into my studio apartment, we have mainly been living off of his student loan and the money I make doing voice-overs for a cartoon character on public television, a little girl with big freckles who talks a lot about sharing. I am also the voice of more than one letter of the alphabet on a show called *Julio's Alphabet City*. And then there are the pornographic voice-overs: just some moaning and groaning and a few dirty words delivered in whispery breath into a microphone, while a bored sound engineer, a struggling comedian, sits drinking his chocolate milk from a carton and reading Freud's *Jokes and Their Relation to the Unconscious*. But what used to be a silly affair has now become a numbing task, relieved only by the uncontrollable giggle fits the sound guy and I break into when I make a mistake in the copy. Like "twits" for "tits"—*"feel my twits."* That one caused a seizure.

Each week I look for work on the stage, a mostly uninspired task. The last play I was in was supposed to be a slice of life in a small Texas town. I could not figure out why it was called *The Lonely Hero,* but each and every cast member felt sure it was their character who was the lonely hero. My character was shot dead at the end of the first act by a crazy gas station attendant who had always been in love with her. I was sure that she was not the lonely hero. Though to be truthful, there was one night, right before the blackout, as I lay on stage bleeding to death, that I thought for just a moment that I might be the lonely hero.

Audiences left confused. Reviews were not good.

I go to an audition where they tell me I have a very specific quality. Also, they say, they don't like it.

At the gym a girl from the New York City Ballet says that winter into summer is the hardest transition to make. Everything expands and gets kind of puffy; that is why everybody feels like shit.

From the street I call Lenny. I don't plan to call. It is never planned.

"I have a very specific puffy quality," I say.

"In that case you better come up," he tells me.

Lenny ushers me in and closes the door to his office.

His staff loves this kind of thing, a visit from a girl-friend, or a former girlfriend, drama in the middle of the day. Lenny looks warm in his clothing made of substantial fabrics: wide wale corduroy trousers, a fisherman's sweater, hand knit in the thickest, most luxurious kind of wool.

I reach down and pat Folly, Lenny's panting yellow Labrador retriever.

"If I wag my tail will you pat me, too," Lenny says.

"Please," I say, "don't start wagging your tail."

Lenny knows I can easily picture him wiggling around, shaking his rear end all over the room. He is capable of large and embarrassing gestures that are meant to make me laugh against my will. I feel sure that he does not tease the others this way. He shows mercy on them. But then, they are cheerful girls. It is my gloominess that poses a challenge to Lenny. It is my long, serious face. "You know," I've told him, "other people think I'm a really fun person." "Oh, sure," he'll say back, and perform some undignified gesture, like he'll lift up my shirt and make a big farting noise on my bare stomach with his mouth. "No really," I'll say, still arguing, still way too serious, "it's you who makes me this way. It's you."

"All right," Lenny says, "I won't wag my tail, but only because I don't want to chase you away."

The phone on Lenny's desk begins to ring.

"Let's get out of here," he says. Lenny lives above the store, as he calls it, in the same building where he keeps his office.

"Okay," I say, "but just to talk."

But there is kissing in the elevator, kissing that I feel in my stomach, in my thighs.

Upstairs we make love quickly, and afterward Lenny draws my body into his.

"How was the birthday dinner?" he asks.

"Could we please not talk about that," I say.

"Sure," he says. And then, "But I'd hate to lay odds on this thing."

"Not true," I say. "You'd love to lay odds on this thing, or *any* thing."

"All right," he says, "ten to one then."

"That's all you know."

"Fine," he says, "but I give the whole idiotic business about two more weeks."

"Two more weeks and then what?" I say, wriggling out of his grasp. "I'm going to come back to you so you can get a pinched nerve in your neck every time I bring up the relationship?"

"Hey," he says, "my pinched nerves aren't funny."

"Of course not," I say, beginning to laugh.

"But, ornithology students," he says, exasperated. "You might as well take a fucking trip on the *Titanic*."

"That's not fair," I say.

"You think I give a shit what's fair," he says, "I'm fighting for my life here."

We are both silent, surprised by the seriousness of Lenny's admission and all that it may imply.

"Come back to me," he says, pulling my body back up against his, "we'll go to France."

"You should have married me," I say.

"I could change," he says. "Changing is not out of the question here."

"And what are the odds of that?"

Outside Lenny's enormous bedroom window the afternoon sky turns a darker shade of gray. Soon I will be shivering in some unheated grocery market, staring at tables of hosed-down lettuce heads, wondering what to make Sandy for dinner, and Lenny will be showering and dressing for a date with someone very pretty. He'll be off to the opening of a show, or a fund-raiser for some Democratic city politician, his tuxedo fitting his body perfectly, making him more handsome than he really is.

"It will rain of course," I say.

"Why of course?" he asks me.

"The sky always darkens when illicit love is made."

"It's true," he says, tightening his hold on my body. "Even in all my clumsiness, I know that much."

"You want to know a secret?" Sandy says. We are lying in the dark. "When you saw me, that first time at the Food Emporium, it wasn't an accidental meeting."

"No?"

"No," he says, "I only looked as though I were benignly stocking the shelves."

"And what were you really doing?"

"Lying in wait."

"Is this a little story?" I ask, hoping it will not be a confession of any kind.

"I came to New York to find you," he says. "School was for show, a viable cover."

"Does that mean this is not a little story?"

"It's a big story," he says. "I knew where you lived of course, and I knew that one day you'd come into the supermarket on my shift. I only had to wait two weeks."

Somewhere I knew this. "Is that the end of the story?" I ask.

"I hope not," he says.

On the weekends Sandy cooks omelets. He stands at the stove, still wearing the brilliant yellow sweatshirt he goes running in, beating the eggs lightly, and folding in mushrooms, green peppers, and grated cheese.

We eat and then wash the dishes together. Sandy washes, I dry.

"I saw something weird yesterday," he tells me.

"What?" I ask, toweling down a wet plate and placing it into the rack.

"I saw a beautiful woman in the subway drop her sunglasses onto the tracks."

"How beautiful?" I ask.

"Well, very beautiful in fact," he says. "And a young student-looking guy actually jumps down onto the tracks and retrieves the sunglasses."

"That's gallant," I say, wondering if the student guy isn't actually Sandy.

"So he hands this beautiful woman her glasses and says, 'Are you a model?' And she gives him this sneer and tells him, 'Why don't you get a face.' "

"Get a face?" I ask.

"Yeah, 'get a face.' "

"I don't even know what that means," I say.

"Me either, but I feel like writing a poem about it," Sandy says. "Facelessness, the getting of a face. Maybe I don't have a face."

"Please," I say, "on top of everything else do not become a poet."

"What's that supposed to mean?" he says, turning off the running water.

"Nothing. A poet is a hard thing to be is all."

"Hey," he says, going into the bathroom for a shower, "get a face."

Sandy studies all day on Saturdays. He sits in the corner with all of his books spread out in front of him while I go grocery shopping at the Food Emporium.

Someone from my acting class is beginning to make it big. She's lying languidly on her side in a national magazine, covering two whole pages like a centerfold. I am thrilled just to have been nominated, she says. *Cannes was such a total trip.* She never comes to acting class anymore. Her boots are red and look Italian. Red, soft, buttery, and *Italian*.

I fold the magazine shut quickly, as though I have seen something I should not have, some pornography, some fierce longing within myself.

I place it back in the rack.

In aisle one, near the salad bar, I think of the night I ran into Sandy. This is where he saw me arranging the greens and the vegetables on a plastic tray, prettily, to make it look artful, to make it mean something. Salad for one in New York City.

Tuna fish is on sale and I watch in a trance as can after can takes its bumpy ride down the black conveyor belt at the checkout counter.

"Honey," Sandy says, taking the grocery bags from my arms. "Did you know that the ostrich may be descended from some kind of dinosaur. New findings. Awesome implications," he says, shaking his head. "Poetic really."

"What?" I say, stacking cans of tuna fish in the cabinet.

"It's just that large birds like the ostrich may be the link between, say, a tiny little sparrow and a dinosaur." He wraps his arms around me and squeezes. He is always grabbing at me, nuzzling me, squeezing a little too hard and cutting off my circulation.

"Stop grabbing me," I say. "You're always grabbing me, always clutching on to me."

"What the hell is the matter with you?" he says, backing away from me.

"I wish it were all in retrospect, that's what's the matter with me," I say. "You know, I could be cute in an interview, too. I could say quotable things. I could make it sound like living on nothing had been a whole lot of fun."

"What's wrong?" he says, worry furrowing his brow.

"I'm tired of the way I live," I say.

"Oh, sweetheart," he says soothingly, "it's only for

a couple more years. We just have to tighten our belts for a couple more years."

"Stop," I say. "I hate that expression. I don't want to tighten anything. I'm already as tight and cramped and pinched as I could ever get. I'm trying to expand," I say, flinging my arms out wide. "I want to paint and act and sing. I am the kind of girl who is trying to *expand*."

"Look," he says, his mouth serious and tight, "I've tried to think of some way to get through school faster. I've gone over it a million times in my head, and there just isn't. There just plain isn't."

"You could try studying instead of writing poetry," I say. "Or else you could try taking your poetry seriously and stop skulking around about it."

He looks suddenly ashamed and I see him as a boy of twelve or thirteen, toting his viola to school, red-faced and defiant. I have known him since forever.

"Am I holding you up?" Sandy shouts.

"Yes," I shout back.

"I'm sorry if you're stuck waiting for a deadbeat like me. I'm so fucking sorry if you're stuck waiting for a *loser* like me."

Three cans of tuna fish tumble from my arms as I run past Sandy and into the bathroom. I slam the door hard. There is nowhere else to go but into this bathroom, no other door to shut against each other but the bathroom door.

I sit down on the edge of the bathtub and wait to see if Sandy will leave. I don't know what Sandy does when we are in a fight; we've never really been in a fight.

Then all is quiet until I hear Sandy as he lets his body slide along the wall outside the door. I can picture him sitting out there, his elbows resting on his knees.

"I could paint the walls," I hear him say after a long silence in which I listen to the water from the bathtub faucet drip. "I could paint each wall a different color," he goes on. "Any color you want the walls to be, I could paint them that color."

I cannot help but picture those birds, those red-tailed hawks, nestling up there on 112th Street, here in this of all cities, amid the carbon monoxide, against pitiful odds. I think of a song I remember from my childhood. "What kind of an animal are you?" it went.

"I'm not a bird," I say.

"True," he says, "but in your case I'm willing to overlook it."

Slowly I open the bathroom door. There it is, the sweetness in Sandy's face. It's the sweetness that made me remember that I had potential for sweetness, too. It is there in his wide-set eyes, as sure as a scientific fact.

FAITH

The angel Gabriel, winged, bronze, and nearly ten feet high, is heralding something. What he is heralding as he stands guard, trumpet in hand, on the cathedral's rooftop, Sandy has no idea. Sandy is a Protestant of some kind or other, but he has been raised by atheists, parents who believe in logic, chaos, science, and good deeds. On school forms that asked his religion, his mother always told him to write "unaffiliated Protestant," which various teachers seemed either not to comprehend or to find very funny.

Sandy is not the only man who sits on a bench at 112th Street and Amsterdam Avenue, on the south side of the Cathedral of Saint John the Divine. But he is the only man who sits with a set of binoculars. He is not sure why the other men have chosen this particular spot, but he is sure of his own purpose. He is carefully noting the activity of a couple of red-tailed hawks, *Buteo jamaicensis,* Audubon plate no. 28, who are building a nest above a bas-relief of an angel. Another angel. What angel he does not know of course, being, as he is, so perpetually unaffiliated.

He has moved out of Faith's apartment and back into his room at Columbia where he is hoping the arrival of the summer term will never come. His housing is contingent on his continued enrollment in the university and soon—when? dates are getting mixed up in his head—he will have to register for classes or be evicted. Still, he feels he can no more leave his hawk-watch and affiliate himself with the banality of things like homework than he can fly. And no, he cannot fly. If he could fly, he would definitely know it by now, as many times as he has imagined the ability, dreamed of the experience, or, as a child, tried to will it into being, jumping out of a tree or off of the well-house roof, and so on. Many attempts took place before the age of reason, which in his particular case seemed to come on the late side.

Sandy is low on money. He is working only a few days a week for a guy named Wallace, who picks up jobs here and there remodeling apartments. Still, he allows himself one cup of thick European coffee and one gooey cheese Danish per day from the Hungarian pastry shop on Amsterdam, across from the Cathedral of Saint John the Divine. He has brought his binoculars along as usual, and with his coffee and his Danish he maneuvers a place on the bench beside the other men who habituality sit here in their ragged pants and old wool overcoats.

It is April now and the hawks are nearly done laying down the nest's superstructure and lining its interior with bark from a large linden tree that grows on the cathedral grounds. Soon they will be done building and mating and will enter the nest-sitting phase. Sandy carries his copy of *Birds of North America* with him, which he reads during the lulls in the hawk's activity. All other reading material seems pointless to him now, or overblown and filled with needless information and trivial detail. He thumbs through the book, gazing at entries he has had memorized since the second grade. I want to be an ornithologist, he told his teacher. What's that? she asked.

The female hawk sits on the nest waiting for the male to swoop down and make love to her. Sandy watches the coupling through his binoculars. Red-tailed hawks are not urban dwellers, and they have never, to his extensive knowledge, set up housekeeping in the city. These red-tailed hawks nesting here in this strange environment fill him with hope for a nest full of blue spotted eggs, for something miraculous and out of context. A nest full of blue spotted eggs would definitely be a sign. He would take it as a sign.

He came to New York to be with Faith, a girl from his hometown in Virginia, a girl he grew up with and had loved for as long as he could remember. Faith, and no other thing, was the passion of his life; she surpassed even birds, even rare or particularly majestic birds, even birds whose mighty wingspans filled him with awe.

Even as a child he felt this way, and knew for this reason that it was possible for a child to feel true passion. It was Faith's image that had sustained him through the boredom of his tour in the army, a particularly alcohol-soaked stint in the Peace Corps, and all the time he'd drifted around in between the two. But now she would have nothing more to do with him. He lacked ambition for one thing and she had always been full of it. She was trying to make it as an actress and he was like a weight around her neck, she said. "You're a drowning man," she said to him. She shook her head slowly, as though the thought of him made her tired. She said more, but he can't bear to think of those last few weeks before she kicked him out of her apartment. Now he sleeps as much as possible. He smokes pot and drinks beer. He eats Franco-American spaghetti out of the can with his only fork. He watches the red-tailed hawks build their nest. He tries to think of nothing at all, not even his hometown, which is Faith's hometown, too. There, she grows in the grass. She lives in the trees.

One of the men on the bench wakes suddenly from a morning nap. He mutters to himself, something about Susan—are you Susan?—and wanders off onto the cathedral grounds. Sandy decides these are the kind of men you would move away from at a lunch counter, greasy-haired, unshaven, talking to themselves. He might move away himself (God, the smell sometimes) if this were not the perfect place in all of New York City for observing the wonder of the red-tailed hawks.

Sandy looks up at the hawks and wonders how much of a choice you have in determining who you become. He's heard of people who have traveled all over the world only to end up in the house they grew up in, dying in the bed they slept in as a child. Where is he headed? Though he doesn't like to think about it, he finds that the question, particularly here on the bench, tends to hurl itself at him, a cosmic lob. He bats it back into the universe like an errant tennis ball.

Through his binoculars he spots the male winging his way back to the female, a large rat, a particularly choice offering, dangling from his beak. The female sits on the edge of her nest devouring the creature. Sandy watches the carnage with growing excitement. Something big for the lifelong bird-watcher he is, as momentous a sighting as you are likely to get. "This is some serious shit," he says to no one in particular. He knows. But he can't stop himself from speaking his thoughts aloud. "This is *life*, man," he announces.

Wallace never asks Sandy questions about his life and Sandy appreciates that fact. Wallace Takihiro, the guy Sandy works for, is a Japanese-American who has chosen unequivocally to emphasize his Japanese side. He is about thirty, Sandy's age, and always wears his straight black hair in a samurai knot on the top of his head. The rest of Wallace's crew is made up of Wallace devotees and hangers-on, guys Wallace has known since high school who clearly worship him—the cult of Wallace, Sandy calls them.

"This isn't the place I'd have if I inherited twenty million bucks," says Wallace.

Wallace has gotten a job redoing the kitchen of a surprisingly modest two-bedroom duplex on the Upper West Side.

"This chick is the heiress to a beer-bottling fortune," he says, pointing to a photograph of the apartment's owner, an heiress on horseback. It is impossible to tell from the blurry photograph what she actually looks like. She is frozen in motion, navigating a glorious jump, her face twisted with effort and concentration.

"We used to paint billboards together in Times Square. It gets fucking freezing up there," says Wallace. "We had electric socks."

"No shit?" says Sandy, impressed.

"Now she's an alternate on the Olympic equestrian

team," says Wallace, ripping up a long piece of linoleum from the kitchen floor, "and one fierce chick."

Sandy wonders if Wallace intends him to believe
that he has slept with the heiress and decides that Wallace intends him to believe just that. He admires Wallace's vigilance in keeping up the Wallace mystique,
admires this kind of attention to persona that seems to
come so naturally to New Yorkers and is so foreign to
him. He observes, he marvels even, but he cannot learn.
It is not in him.

Wallace is tall and has been able to make a lot of
money modeling in Japan, enough to buy up a couple
of run-down buildings and turn them into fashionable
galleries. Like Sandy he is good with his hands, but
unlike Sandy, Wallace is entrepreneurial, with an eye
for turning rubbish into cash. Sandy has witnessed the
Wallace hustle, has watched him use his exotic looks
and his low-watt Eastern charisma to get high-paying
renovation jobs. He has watched with interest as Wallace initiative is transformed into Wallace success. Wallace is not a hawk-watcher glued to a nest in the wall
of a cathedral, or a writer of poetry, another of Sandy's
pursuits, which Sandy now determines has gotten him
exactly nowhere.

On the other hand, it is he, Sandy, and not Wallace,
who is in on a rare secret, which he holds to his heart
like a lover, as he rips up linoleum and pulls old cabi-

nets from the heiress's kitchen wall. The eggs have been laid, and soon, in a couple of weeks maybe, the eggs will hatch. Hatchlings. Baby hawks! Out of context. A miracle. It boggles the mind, this kind of offering, a gift like this. In the morning, the only dreams Sandy can remember are dreams of the hawks and their spotted blue eggs.

The day wears on, the rhythm of the labor pleasantly steady, and from time to time as he works, Sandy steals illicit glances at the photograph. *One fierce chick.* The heiress's leg in the stretchy white riding pants is turning him on, which surprises him. She is, after all, a woman, and not an egg or a nest, or even a red-tailed hawk.

Summer school begins, he supposes anyway. He sees people milling about with their knapsacks and books. The Hungarian pastry shop is busy again and it takes longer than usual to get his coffee in the morning. He has had to forgo his pastry for lack of funds and has brought along a peanut butter and jelly sandwich assembled at home.

Sandy makes his way to the bench where he is stopped, stunned by what he sees. One of the men on the bench sits holding a cardboard sign, which has been pulled from a stake in the ground. It reads: WARNING. POISON. QUINTOX HAS BEEN PLACED IN RAT HOLES THROUGHOUT THE GROUNDS.

Sandy races to find the church groundkeeper, his head filled with plans for an all-out campaign to have the poison removed. He will get some big-time ornithologists from the university and the Museum of Natural History to call . . . who?—somebody, a bishop. He will get the Department of Environmental Protection involved. He will find and remove the rat poison himself.

He is breathless and babbling by the time he finds the groundskeeper in charge, a gray-haired Puerto Rican man who calls him "son" and advised him in fractured English to calm down. The groundskeeper, it turns out, is easily convinced to remove the poison for the good of nature.

"Yes, exactly, for the good of nature," Sandy repeats. He is beginning to catch his breath, to allow the panicky sensation to leave his body. "For the good of nature," he says again. But in the hours that follow he remains gripped by a sickening sense of dread. What if one of the red-tails has eaten a poisoned rat? How will its reproductive system be affected? If the birds are poisoned, he is helpless to unpoison them. Instead he decides to poison himself. With pot and beer. With Jack Daniel's. With caffeine and cigarettes. With anything he can find. How he would love to add a poisonous woman to the mix.

As his days on the watch continue, he finds he is more or less able to block the poison rat-hole incident from his mind, a practice of deliberately inducing amnesia, which he notices he is growing alarmingly good at.

An official-looking letter arrives. He finds it tucked under the door, waiting for him to come home. They know he hasn't registered for classes, the letter says. Time to get out, Buddy, or words to that effect.

He opens a can of baked beans stolen from a high-priced supermarket on upper Broadway, and sits down at his desk. He doodles some birds on a notepad. Pelicans, he thinks, giving them long, exaggerated legs. He gets a cartoon strip going. With each panel a small speck of soil accumulates, forming a ball that finally forms the earth. "The Birth of Dirt," he titles it. He reaches for the eviction notice and writes on the back in large block letters: HATCH DAY IS IMMINENT. He places the notice in an envelope and uses his last stamp to mail it back to Campus Housing.

Since he has not known Wallace since high school, he is low man on the totem pole as far as picking up work is concerned, which is fair enough, except for the fact that he is running so low on money. So he is relieved when Wallace calls, offering him a day's work on the heiress's kitchen. Plus, working in the heiress's apartment is not at all unpleasant. The apartment itself is airy and filled with plants and unusual paintings, in contrast with his university housing, which is dark and small and cluttered with his unwashed laundry and heaps of musty secondhand books, pizza boxes and beer cans, unemptied ashtrays.

At the end of the day Sandy offers to stay behind and clean up the sawdust. He had noted that her freezer was full of frozen dinners, and later he plans to heat up a couple of Lean Cuisines. It will take more than one of them to fill him up, they are so small. How can women subsist on such minuscule rations? With the rest of the crew gone, he turns on the oven and throws in a couple of the dinners.

He is sweeping up the kitchen floor, his mind pleasantly occupied with the fact that he is saving himself a few dollars on dinner or the stress of having to shoplift canned food, when he hears a key turning in the locked door.

He specifically heard Wallace say that she was at her horse farm in Connecticut, but now the heiress is standing in front of him. He is face-to-face with the mythical goddess on horseback, the owner of the stolen Lean Cuisines.

"You better be one of the workmen," she says, dropping her bags onto the floor.

"That's me," he says, trying to sound reassuring.

She looks frazzled, her face puffy, her eyes red and glazed, as though she has been crying. She is not nearly as pretty as he has fantasized, but she is younger than he'd imagined, in her late twenties, he guesses. Her thick brown hair is cropped off bluntly at her chin and she is dressed in cutoff jeans and a denim jacket.

They look at one another a moment and Sandy feels his face go red with shame. All he can think of are his contraband Lean Cuisines, filling the apartment with their food smells, exposing him for the lowly, thieving personage he is.

"Is something cooking?" she asks.

He nods. "Lean Cuisine," he says.

"Are you stealing my food?" she asks.

He can still muster a smile, he guesses. Probably, he still can. It's not like he never had any charm whatsoever. At one time he definitely had a little charm. There had been seductions. He had seduced. Though it is possible that he is not the same man who once pulled off various seductions, possible that the man with that knack is long gone, a ghost, he decides to attempt to conjure up a vestige of the lover he once was. He decides to try a smile.

"I hope you're not going to call the police," he says.

"I guess it could be worse," she says. Is she smiling back? "You could be riffling through my underwear drawer."

At one time he had been downright courtly. He smiles a little more.

"Is there another one of those things in the freezer?" she asks. "I'm so hungry, I'm dizzy. I think my electrolytes are about to go out."

She marches past him unself-consciously—she's used to him already—and up the spiral staircase to the second floor. "I'm taking a shower till dinner," she calls.

Alone in the kitchen, Sandy continues to sweep up debris, more to prove that he is working than anything. He cannot recall ever having wanted to leave a place more in his life, but now with his dinner in the oven, her dinner, too, he would look even more like the criminal he is. And something else too, and worse even than thievery where he comes from: he might appear *ungracious*.

She reemerges wrapped in a long white terry-cloth bathrobe. Her hair is wet from the shower and she is wearing a pair of chic but serious-looking horn-rimmed glasses. He inhales her clean scent as she walks past him. She smells nice, feminine, of soap and shampoo.

"I've got a bottle of wine in the fridge," she says, "would you mind getting it?"

To Sandy's surprise the two of them simply gather up some glasses and silverware, sit down at the dining-room table together, and begin to eat.

She takes a long sip of wine.

"I'm Frances," she tells him. "What's your name?"

"Sandy," he says.

"Let me ask you something, Sandy," she says. "What would you do if you were supposed to go to a wedding with someone you were seeing, and they missed it. Just didn't show up, and claimed it had something to do with some bullshit about a fucked-up motorcycle? What if pretty much everything that came out of this person's mouth was a goddamned lie." She begins to cry and wipes her nose on the sleeve of her bathrobe. "Huh?" she says, removing her glasses.

"Don't cry," he says helplessly.

"Got any pot?" she says, sniffing. She pushes her half-eaten dinner away from her.

"Not on me," he says.

"Can you get me some?" she asks.

"Probably," he says.

"Wait," she says, getting up from the table, "I do have some. Hold on."

He watches her climb the stairs to her bedroom, then quickly seizes the chance to bolt down the rest of his pathetic and ill-gotten meal. He eats quickly, still wondering how a full-grown woman can live on such tiny portions.

Frances reemerges carrying two joints. She sits on the couch with her feet tucked under her and lights one up, inhaling deeply.

"Want some?" she says. The act of inhaling and exhaling, the breathing itself, seems to calm her. Sandy joins her on the couch and takes the joint.

"I like your tattoo," he says, gesturing toward the green lizard, which runs the length of her slender ankle.

She asks where he's from. "You have a nice accent," she says. She seems to be looking at him for the first time since she walked through the door.

"*You* have the accent," he tells her, "I'm from Virginia."

"Where in Virginia?" she asks. "I spend a lot of time down there on the circuit."

"A very small town," he says, "nowhere near horse country." He takes another hit off the joint and conjures a remarkably clear picture of the town, a wooded grove with its hundreds of sheltering trees. It is always there, in his mind, in his heart—however you want to think of it—there inside him with more texture, more color, more sound than his immediate surroundings here in New York. At night, like a hawk, he flies above its wooded acres. He soars through its open fields. He perches on the rooftops of its peculiar old houses.

Frances lights the other joint. "Not much of a city boy," she says. She moves closer to him and he automatically puts his arm around her. He realizes he has not touched another human being in many months, not since Faith tried awkwardly to hug him good-bye and he stood there, arms rigid at his side, frozen with grief. Now he feels awed by the cool, damp nape of Frances's neck. Frances. He likes the name.

"You know, I think I would like to riffle through your underwear drawer," he says.

"Oh, really," she says and they both start to laugh.

"Yes," he says, he's high now, "I'd like to run my fingers through every single pair of your beautiful, silky panties."

"Panties," she says, snorting, "panties is the funniest word I can think of."

"Panties," he says. It is funny.

"Panties," says Frances, lying back on the couch and holding her stomach as she gasps for air.

"Panties," he says, propping himself on top of her. They begin to kiss. "You have beautiful legs," he says, "I've been looking at your picture on the wall."

"I have to have a good body," she tells him, her laughter subsiding now, "I don't have a pretty face."

"Bullshit," he says. Her face is a little odd, a little asymmetrical, but he can see how if you loved her, she would look beautiful.

"You don't have to give me compliments," she says, "I know what I look like."

"Do you?" he says, giving her more of his body weight. He wants those legs of hers wrapped around his waist. He pulls the belt of her robe loose and begins to touch her warm, smooth body. They kiss very deeply, urgently, and Sandy begins to feel as though he has fallen into a dream. He could love this woman, he thinks. She needs love.

She has reached her hands underneath Sandy's T-shirt and is touching the bare skin of his back when the phone begins to ring. They both jump, then sit up suddenly, caught. They listen as the machine picks up the call. It is a man's voice, low and remorseful, and Frances leaps to pick up the receiver.

She turns away and speaks quietly, her back to him now. "Nothing," she says a few times, and, "Okay."

She places the phone back on the hook and straightens her bathrobe. "That was my boyfriend. We had a big fight. I think I told you about that," she says, tying her belt. "Anyway, now he's on his way into the city." He watches her walk to the dining-room table and pick up her serious-looking glasses. "Don't leave mad," she says, not looking at him, "just leave."

Sandy walks up Broadway, passing men in doorways huddled in their filthy sleeping bags. It has rained, and even though the streets are slick and the air is damp, the city does not seem cleansed. The sky is a strange plum color, filled with polluted clouds. Near the subway station at Seventy-second Street a man tries to sell raw T-bone steaks out of a cooler. Stolen meat.

He walks until he finds himself in front of Faith's apartment on West Eighty-sixth Street. From the bus stop across the street he can see the bluish cast of a TV screen and a flicker of light on the wall every now and then. He knows she has trouble falling asleep and likes to watch talk shows into the night, as far into the night as they'll go sometimes. He used to tell her little stories that would put her right to sleep. He'd stroke her hair. It couldn't have been all bad.

A flicker again. The bluish color. But that is all.

After a glorious spring full of breezy days and low barometric pressure, the weather has turned humid and sticky. Bus fumes linger in the air and the garbage on the street smells rancid. Sandy waits for the nest full of eggs to hatch. The day is coming.

The university's housing office urges him to make some meaningful contact regarding his plans to vacate the premises. Sandy writes back what he considers to be a very coherent and remorseful letter regarding his failure to register for summer classes. He has experienced a death in the family, he writes, and he has had to shuttle back and forth between New York and Virginia to take care of the many details that death has wrought. He likes that part, *death has wrought*. At the end of the letter he is upbeat and optimistic about beginning the second half of the summer term, and full of apologies about his failure to properly communicate with the housing office regarding his plans.

Writing the letter causes him to actually feel upbeat and optimistic about the second half of the summer term, and as he finishes it, he feels, for the first time in months, that he will be able to concentrate on school. He begins to look forward to the formal study of ornithology. He even takes some notes for a paper he is planning to write on urban wildlife. He cuts back on his drinking, and with no conscious effort, he cuts back on his sleeping, too. In fact, he feels unable to sleep very much at all, and either reads all night (he has missed reading) or runs, remembering high school and the cross-country team, forgetting everything.

Though the normal egg-sitting time, twenty-eight to thirty-two days, has passed by two weeks, Sandy sees no real cause for alarm. If not today then tomorrow, Sandy tells himself, as dusk begins to fall and there is not too much more to see through his binoculars. If not today then tomorrow. We're dealing with some unusual circumstances here. It's not as though this is their natural habitat. If not today then tomorrow. Out loud, to himself, he continues to repeat this line like a mantra. He does that now, all the time. He sputters things out loud and has ceased to give any kind of shit about it at all.

The first week in June arrives.

"Stopped sitting on the nest," says a voice. Sandy turns to look at the man beside him, a grizzled sight. It's the lunatic who asks, Where's Susan?, and wanders off alone. Listening to a lunatic. What does a lunatic, a man who has walked through a rip in time and space know of blue spotted eggs and hatchlings?

But Sandy watches through his binoculars as the childless birds flutter about helplessly, flying from the roof down to the scaffolding and then onto a ledge of one of the high cathedral windows.

He watches the birds stare eerily inside the cathedral windows, as though they want in. He wonders what they would look like from the other side, to a person who is on the other side of those long, elegant windows. Funny, he has never thought to actually go inside the cathedral. For the unaffiliated, there is no urgent need.

He walks around to the cathedral's entrance. COME IN AND PRAY, says a sign, and he cannot remember receiving so welcome an invitation. He pulls on an enormous wood door and finds it opens easily, with nothing more than a gentle tug.

Sandy steps inside and is struck by the coolness of the stone walls all around him and the sudden, overwhelming absence of the city's loud, persistent din. The inside of the cathedral is enormous yet hushed, and tranquil beyond anything he could have imagined. He feels an urge to pray, to reach upward somehow, toward something. He wants to pray and he has no idea how to pray. But as he walks down the cavernous corridor a sense of wholeness finds him; it is familiar, too, ancient and peaceful, as in one of his flying dreams.

He knows he will not be staying for the summer term, or any other term that might follow. A *term*, the idea itself begins to seem absurd, arbitrary, like a sentence he has imposed upon himself for his many, many sins, and one from which it is now so easy to be freed. For looking up at the ceiling's massive arches of stone, he sees trees. He sees the trees of his hometown in Virginia, sees their branches reach heavenward, and then bend gracefully overhead to form a great cathedral of their own. He is inside it now, a sanctuary of strong, sheltering branches, and cool, green leaves.

WINGING
IT

Her hand on his brow had never soothed him. In fact, he couldn't remember her ever once actually placing her hand on his brow, couldn't remember her smoothing his hair or any like gesture. And yet, the image of Faith's cool hands on his forehead kept returning to him, her messy, white hands, slim and tapered, their fingernails embedded with colored chalk, paint, or clay. He kept thinking of her hands.

Lenny sat in his office staring at the phone. His life was falling apart, he'd tell her, which incidentally was not untrue. Barring an eleventh-hour deal with investors, he would be forced to file for bankruptcy. Still true. The Wyoming, his high rise on Fifty-seventh Street, was supposed to bail him out of the mess he was in, but the real-estate market had abruptly fallen apart. People were staying put, cutting back, eating in, and no one was buying, not luxury they weren't. He had financed The Wyoming by borrowing heavily against his existing properties. A strategy like that can work during a boom. But the boom had fizzled. Now, he was nearly ten million in the hole, small potatoes compared to what was happening to some other guys. Still they were *his* potatoes, his only potatoes.

Maybe he should have stayed in the music business. It was capricious, unstable, but at least you could feel a certain thrill at finding new talent, and you could always hope. What could he hope for when high-ceilinged apartments with marble tile, Jacuzzis, and sundecks sat unoccupied? He continued to stare at his telephone, fearing another night of panic, of waking up drenched in his own cold sweat, his heart hammering wildly.

What had happened to the days when a plan presented itself with all the beauty of a full-blown symphony, at once inspired and precise? He felt a surge and dialed Faith's number. Like all truly good plans this plan would be absurdly simple. He loved her, and he would tell her so, that's all. He might tell her so ceremoniously over dinner. Or maybe it should pop out spontaneously while driving to or from the restaurant. He wasn't sure. But with his aim clear, he would be poised, ready at any moment to wing it beautifully. He would offer her something this time, marriage maybe. Okay, sure, he was willing to go that far.

He spoke into her machine, reasonably sure that she was there, listening measuredly, her arms folded defensively against her body.

"If you're there," he began, "I was just thinking of you."

He waited a moment for her to pick up and when

she did not he hung up the phone. He was laying the groundwork. It was a good start.

He glanced up at the top of the tallest ficus tree. A couple of leaves had turned yellow and he wondered when they would drop to the ground. Soon he would be gone from this office. And though he did not want to leave his magnificent cathedral windows, the ones he designed himself, some guy, some tax lawyer, was offering him sixty-five thousand a year for it, and right now he was in no position to turn down sixty-five thousand a year. There would not be room for his art collection in his new office; the canvases were very large. The new office was low-ceilinged and poorly ventilated, a mean little closet of a space, and he anticipated feeling pinched in there after ten prosperous years of watching his ficus tree grow and grow to where its leaves now grazed the twenty-foot ceiling. He had always liked to imagine a giraffe nibbling there. Plenty of room for wildlife.

His phone rang. It was his private line, the one that bypassed his receptionist, and he dove for the receiver.

"Don't you know times have changed," Faith said, "rich boyfriends are out."

"What's in?" he asked. Her tone was cheerful. He was taken off guard.

"Extreme caution," she said. "Extreme caution is making a comeback."

"But you were never the trendy type," he said. "Besides, rich boyfriends are classic, they never go out of style."

She laughed, rather musically, which surprised him. Faith was a brooder most of the time, and when she quit brooding, she cried, and was mostly impossible to console.

"Sorry I didn't pick up," she said, "I'm covered in paint."

He had cautioned her strongly against splitting her focus between her acting career and this urge to paint, but now he liked this image of Faith—"covered in paint." He liked the fact that she never gave up, even when it seemed to him that the things she pursued brought her no pleasure whatsoever. She could be inhumanly patient. He admired that about her, and he had meant for some of it to rub off on him. He had begun to notice how superficially he went about things. He liked to dream up big projects, but when it came to overseeing the details of an operation, he tended to leave the follow-through to others. The inspiration that had given birth to his buildings, his restaurants, and his record albums was beginning to seem like little more than a flaw in his character.

"How about a little dinner," he offered, "a little holiday dinner with an old friend?"

"Well," she hesitated, smart girl. A picture of her

running down the street flashed into his mind. He was chasing her and she was screaming over her shoulder something about how her brother, a member of the U.S. armed forces, and an old boyfriend of hers from her hometown would come up here to New York and beat the shit out of him if he didn't leave her alone. The incident had occurred only six months ago, but somehow it sat in his brain as a much more distant memory. Had he really chased her like that?

"Hey, you got to eat, don't you?" he said.

"Well, yes."

"And by coincidence, I got to eat, too," he said.

He waited for a reply, and as the silence accumulated his apprehension turned to confidence.

"All right, Lenny, I *gotta eat*," she mimicked him, "but do not bother trying to get me drunk. You know I no longer drink alcohol."

"Since when?" he asked. But he knew since when. She claimed to have developed an allergy to alcohol about two years ago, around the time she stopped coming to his company's softball games, around the time she stopped caring if his team lost or won. And now he did not have the team at all. He worked too hard and did not have time for that sort of thing.

"I have always been allergic to alcohol," she said, "I just didn't know it, that's all."

"Well, it seems to me that this allergy to alcohol

came out of nowhere," he said, swiveling irritably in his leather chair.

"Look," she said, exasperated, "my body just can't tolerate the alcohol, okay?"

"Okay, okay," he said, trying to soothe her. The plan. "But you're no fun," he could not resist saying. This allergy to alcohol irritated him beyond belief.

"As you know," she said, "fun isn't really my thing."

It was mid-December and cold enough to snow. Lenny drove up Broadway toward Faith's apartment, wondering why he could not long instead for Noreen, his present girlfriend. Faith was not as pretty as Noreen, and Faith dressed badly. Unless he bought her something nice to wear she ran around in jeans and sweatshirts and was not the kind of girl who looked particularly good dressed like that. Not like Noreen, whose coffee-colored skin and tall, tight body made her look chic in anything. And he really did like Noreen, he liked her tidiness. Even with the amount of professional grooming required for her to go to an audition, she always left the bathroom spotless. She made the bed. She wiped off countertops. She left things tidy. This was unlike Faith who could demolish a bathroom with one quick shower, leaving behind a trail of wet, rumpled towels. He was surprised to find out that he had come to value in a woman such an ordinary trait as tidiness. So now he knew the common truth about himself: tidiness gave him a sense of well-being. But Faith had the hair he loved. Faith's hair felt like silk against his hand. There was power in its gold color, power enough to make him feel hungry almost, filled up with emptiness.

He strained to recognize the old Faith, his Faith, in this confident-looking woman who emerged from her apartment building wrapped up in a long white coat. To support her painting, she had recently begun drawing erotic pictures for a well-known men's magazine. He had bought the magazine once or twice especially to look at her tiny pen and ink drawings, which, she told him, were meant only to fill up space at the end of an article that was too short. The drawings of couples engaged in intercourse looked vaguely oriental and had nothing to do with her real style, but to his surprise, they turned him on just a little. The magazine was paying her pretty well, and she still had her voice-overs. It made him nervous that she had not asked him for any money in over six months. Nothing, not even an emergency loan to pay off an acting teacher or a chiropractor.

"You're looking prosperous," he said.

She smiled and shut the car door.

"I'm doing okay," she said, "I'm getting a lot of voice-overs, plus I sold a painting."

They kissed hello, lightly on the lips. Her cool breath aroused him slightly.

She pulled away quickly. "Sorry," she said, smiling, "I got lipstick on you."

"That white coat must be hard to take care of," he said.

"Yes," she answered, "but the very impracticality of it makes it festive."

Festive. The word made him uneasy. It was not her kind of word at all. She stroked the soft lapel of her coat as if it were a kitten. This disturbed him, her reveling in the luxury of a white coat she could afford herself. He thought of Faith's all-white cat, who more than once had rolled around on unattended pallets of oil paints, and had remained multicolored for months. He started the car, resisting the parental urge to predict that the pure white coat was not long for this unclean city.

"Which painting did you sell?" he asked.

"I got a piece into the small works show and this incredibly beautiful woman who said that she and her husband produce Off-Broadway plays bought it."

"Small works?" he asked. Her work had always been gigantic. Triptychs of large, sheltering trees took up the entire wall space in her downtown studio.

"Yeah," she said, "the piece had to be smaller than twelve square inches."

"Since when have you been doing small pieces?"

"Since I gave up my studio space and started painting in my apartment."

"Faith," he said, "I wish you'd let me keep paying for the space downtown."

"Forget it," she said firmly, "I found having to adapt my work to a small space kind of exciting. I mean, I had this limitation and I found I could still make something. It's a new era, the era of adaptation."

"You really think you're going to get galleries to pay you a studio visit in your Upper West Side apartment?"

"They'll have to," she said.

"Well, you're being very naive, in my opinion. You're not going to get anywhere without a real studio space."

"Hey, Lenny," she said. "I already am somewhere."

He drove through the park where the tree branches near Tavern on the Green had been decorated with tiny white lights. She flicked her hair back in a gesture familiar to him. He felt a pang. He missed her hair long, the way it had run down her back and simply lay flat and shining.

"You cut your hair," he said.

"Yeah," she answered, fluffing it a little. "It's the haircut of my life."

He parked the car and they walked a block or so to the restaurant, a small, elegant place with a woodsy mural covering the wall, lush fruits and vegetables in abundance, nymphs and satyrs cavorting here and there. The maître d' sat them near the back as Lenny had requested. Very expensive restaurants had always pleased Faith and she looked delighted as the waiter dropped her napkin into her lap. He had known other girls like Faith when he was young and managing clubs in the Village, romantics inspired by art, beauty, and glamour, including the kind that only money can buy. He had always liked this kind of girl. This kind of girl made him feel sure of life's infinite potential.

A head waiter about Lenny's age poured the wine.

"None for me," said Faith, holding her palm over the mouth of the glass.

"A little," he coaxed, "to toast the New Year."

"A little," she said, relinquishing her hand.

He noticed a clear chunk of crystal dangling from a thin silver chain around her neck. He wondered if the crystal had some religious symbology, or if it were a fashionable decoration with no meaning at all. He watched it hang there a moment as he tried to remember what he had heard about crystals. They were meant to keep out the bad energy, one of his daughter's friends had told him. They receive radio waves, his daughter had said.

"To the New Year," she said, raising her glass.

The glass and the hanging crystal both caught the light, and he felt the impulse to rip the thing from around her neck. The crystal hung there mocking his plan, a bright insinuation that he would not win her over this time.

"What's wrong?" she asked.

"A couple of business problems," he said, raising his glass and then taking a large sip of his wine. Tomorrow morning if the loan on The Wyoming didn't go through, the wolf, who'd been lurking around outside, could actually come and padlock his office doors.

He managed to smile.

"It's a soft market, right?" she asked.

He hated that expression. It reminded him of a limp prick.

"I'm trying to refinance The Wyoming. It's got me nuts," he said.

"Have you noticed all these new buildings in New York named after states and cities in the Midwest? Can you imagine, Montana is suddenly chic? Not the real Montana of course, but an urban person's idea of Montana, Ralph Lauren's Montana."

"Or Wyoming," he said, glad that the focus of the conversation had shifted away from his impending doom. "What do I know from Wyoming," he said, managing a laugh, "I'm a Jew from New York."

Faith laughed, too, and he chalked up a point for himself. He knew she liked these things about him, his Jewishness and his New Yorkness; his ethnicity and his savvy combined to make him exotic in her eyes. Jews, she said, were so emotionally expressive. She found New York the same way, emotionally expressive. That's why she'd come here from some tiny little town in Virginia or West Virginia, he could never remember which. She liked it when cab drivers screamed at one another. They screamed, she said, and then everything went back to normal. Nobody sulked and feelings were not injured beyond repair. The flow of traffic simply resumed.

The waiter came around and took their order. He poured more wine for Lenny, but Faith brought her hand down fast over the mouth of her wineglass and the waiter returned the bottle to the wine bucket.

"It's just wine, Faith," Lenny said, holding up his glass and taking another sip.

"Wino," she said, which for some reason sounded funny. They both laughed.

"No, I'm serious," she protested. "You're drinking too much."

He threw his arm around her and gave her shoulder a squeeze. He was pleased with the spontaneity of this act, and began rubbing the back of her neck. He inhaled her perfume and noted with pleasure that it was probably the Chanel he had bought her in the giant bottle on his last trip to Paris. She seemed to relax into his touch, and it occurred to him that he couldn't take her back to his place tonight. Noreen's stuff was everywhere, neatly hung, of course, and placed in piles, but very much in evidence. She was gone, out in L.A. for a couple of pilot auditions, and while he couldn't decide if he missed her exactly, without company the penthouse seemed oddly shabby, and drafty, too. He was higher up than other buildings around him and when he looked out a window, there was not one sign of life nearby, only weather. Gusts of wind bumped up against the large picture windows. Sometimes the whole place shuddered and shook and he imagined his apartment was being lifted off of the top of the building. He imagined it spinning through space, the windows like large portholes in a flying ship. Clouds floated by and filled him with feelings of helplessness and distress.

"If you'd help me out," he said into her ear, "I wouldn't have to drink this whole bottle by myself."

"I told you, Lenny, my body can't tolerate the alcohol," she said.

He held on to the thin silver chain, which held that antagonistic little hunk of glass.

"Your body used to tolerate the alcohol pret-ty good," he said.

"Yeah, well, now it doesn't," she said curtly. He could feel her neck muscles stiffen. "Being thirty changes things."

"You're twenty-nine," he said, removing his hand from her neck, and reaching for the wine in its ice bucket nearby. Faith had turned twenty-nine over the summer, but she talked a lot about the experience of being thirty.

"I happen to know you're twenty-nine," he said, "because when you turn thirty, I turn fifty-three, and last time I checked I was still fifty-two."

She ignored him and began eating the mixed greens, which had been sitting in front of her.

Lenny pulled the bottle from the bucket and noticed that small round pieces of ice were stuck to it all over. It looked interesting and reminded him of barnacles he had recently seen while scuba diving in the Caribbean. He had felt peaceful underwater, swimming amid the brightly colored fish, his heavy body buoyed by an ocean of blue water, following Noreen's flipper-covered feet as she swam like a silky little eel.

"Noreen, look," he said, holding the bottle up in the air. He realized his mistake immediately, and hoping Faith had not heard him correctly, he went about pouring himself another glass of wine. But it was too late. It was out—the magic word. *Noreeeeen.* He replaced the bottle and turned toward Faith to assess the damage. She'd fixed her mouth into a pout and pushed her plate away from in front of her.

"I guess you know what you just called me," she said.

"Oh, Jesus, Faith, you're not going to get all upset about that, are you?"

"You don't even know who you're having dinner with," she fumed. "One girl has always been as good as the next."

"Of course I know who I'm having dinner with. It was a slip of the tongue," he said. "That's never happened to you? You never had a slip of the tongue?"

"No, never," she said.

"Oh, come on. It happens to everybody all the time. I call my kids by each other's names all the time. They don't care."

"I bet they *do* care," she said. The angry edges of her voice scraped against him.

"Well, somebody of your intellect shouldn't be upset by such an insignificant slip of the tongue."

"That's where you are so deeply mistaken, Lenny. It's got nothing to do with intellect." Her voice was low but filled with fury. "*You* hurt *my* feelings for the ten millionth time, and now you sit there and tell me I should overcome it with my intellect."

"What do you want from my life?" he pleaded.

"An apology," she demanded.

She sat waiting, her arms folded over her chest, her green eyes narrow and piercing with rage. It seemed she had always been mad at him.

He stalled, taking a large sip of wine. She had gotten up and left him sitting in restaurants before, and right now, she was probably trying to figure out whether she had enough money on her for cab fare home.

"Come on, Faith," he said, soothingly he hoped.

He did not want to be left sitting alone. He knew the maître d'. People at the tables all around him would stare. He'd shrugged off such humiliations before with pretty good grace, joking with the waiter about how touchy women could be, shrugging theatrically for the benefit of people sitting nearby. But tonight he did not feel up to a show of how little he cared if a woman walked out on him.

The waiter appeared carrying hot plates of grilled vegetables and fish. Faith nodded petulantly when the young man asked if she was through with her salad. If she had not gotten up and left him by now, she probably would not do so. The moment to have stormed out of there in a satisfying rage had passed for her, he hoped.

She began to rise.

"I'm going to the ladies' room," she said.

"Your fish will get cold," he said.

"I don't give a fuck," she said back.

That was all the slap in the face he'd receive then, Faith's fish turning cold on the plate next to him; she knew quite well he was of a generation who could not bear wasted food. He should have said he was sorry but she was going to let him off the hook this time, and as he watched her walk through the room full of people, mostly men talking business, he felt grateful to her. He watched men glance up from their conversations. The way she moved had a definite sexual allure, though he could not figure out what precisely made her movements so enticing. Her legs were sturdy and solid, but cute the way a cheerleader's legs were cute, and her upper body was long and graceful, her arms willowy, her fingers long and tapered. Her face looked innocent sometimes and reminded him of Alice in Wonderland, while other times the catlike shape of her eyes made her look feline, and ultimately made her sexier than the ingenue she just missed resembling.

He watched her disappear down a flight of stairs, and the image of her five or six years ago, sitting on the sidelines at the company team's softball games, eased its way pleasantly into his mind. She would watch him play, rather badly, but not because he wasn't a decent athlete, he had been in his time, but because he was at least fifteen years older than the oldest player. Faith wouldn't *root* exactly, but she'd be there, wearing cutoff shorts and sipping diet Coke from a can, and the fact of her being there made a difference in his game. Despite her constant protests that fun was not her thing, she could in fact be fun then. She was the kind of girl who would give a man a blow job in a moving elevator, if she were in a certain mood.

"Are you happy?" she asked, returning to the table.

"Not especially," he answered.

"I thought you'd be happy to know that you can still upset me."

"Don't be ridiculous," he said.

Faith bit into her fish as though she were now very hungry. It satisfied him to watch her eat.

"After all these years, I see you're finally getting gray hairs, Lenny," she said. "Yes, sir, I see plenty of gray hairs." She took another bite of fish. "I hope you realize you're *old now*."

He laughed. "I'm finally becoming respectable," he said. Buoyed, he continued on, "Hey, did I tell you about my plans to open a couple of restaurants in Moscow. I've already had meetings on it and people are excited. I'm getting a really positive response on this one." He was beginning to feel a whole lot better. He wasn't out of the game, not yet. He still had a couple of first-rate ideas to pitch, and in his game, first-rate ideas were it. Everything.

"What about a bistro on the moon?" Faith said, and pausing between her ravenous bites of food, she smiled at him. It was a smile so genuinely warm and filled with affection for him that he was taken off guard. He felt a catch in the back of his throat. He flagged down the waiter and asked him to pick out something for dessert.

"Heavily chocolate," said Faith.

They drove back over to the West Side through the park, where the sight of the white Christmas lights in the trees made him feel light. Faith removed her gloves and he took her hand. She let him hold it there on his thigh as he drove. He thought again of Faith's cool hand smoothing the worry from his brow.

"What are you doing for the holidays?" she asked him.

"Telluride with the kids," he answered.

"*Noreeeen,* too?" she asked.

"No," he assured her as a wave of dread passed through him. This one had developed a keen sense for when a lie was being told. They reached her apartment and he pulled into an available space.

"Well, I suppose I should be flattered," she said,

pulling her hand away from him and fitting it back into its soft pink glove. "You're still bothering to lie to me after all these years."

"I'm not lying," he said. He turned off the ignition and sat with his hands on the steering wheel.

"No, really, it's almost endearing," she said.

"Faith," he said, "I love you."

"Yeah," she said, "but not enough."

He took hold of both of her arms and pulled her body as close to him as he could. It was important that she not leave the car.

"Let go of my coat," she said, struggling to free herself from him.

He could not be hurting her, he thought, not through the thick fabric of that absurd white coat. But before he could make up his mind about it, she was out of his grasp and popping open the car door handle. He pulled the keys from the ignition and stepped from the car onto the sidewalk. Now they stood facing each other in front of her building.

"Lenny," she said, "everything has changed. I'm thirty years old now." She looked him in the face, not unsympathetically, then turned and walked to her door. He watched as she disappeared inside the building.

Go after her, he thought, but his body remained there on the sidewalk. He could get her back for good if he could give up Noreen. But he was not in a position to be giving things up. He had to hold on to the things that he had left, the things that were not volatile.

"You're twenty-nine," he said, though she was well out of earshot now. And then enraged, he yelled it again as loudly as he could, "You're twenty-nine, Faith." He walked to his car and pounded the roof a couple of times, "You're twenty-fucking-nine," he shouted. Her age was a fact, he thought, getting into his car and slamming shut the car door. Her age did not vary with the use of crystals. It could not be altered by allergies to wine and festive white coats. Her age was a fact and he wanted to get the facts absolutely straight.

He started the car and waited to feel some pain in his hands, but it was useless. They were numb with cold.

He pulled out into the street and drove. The stretch of upper Broadway depressed him—too many men on a cold night with rags for shoes—and he began to speed, remembering something Faith had said one time. It was outside her old apartment in Hell's Kitchen, before he had seen to it that she move uptown to a clean place with some real furniture. He was dropping her off, but she hesitated, looking anxious about something.

"I love you," she said. "Don't you love me?"

She was twenty-two and believed in certain absolutes, like the simplicity of equal and requited love.

Now he couldn't fathom it, someone with faith in that kind of love above suspicion.

He came to a red light and stopped. "You're twenty-nine," he said out loud. But the thought brought him no relief this time. Twenty-nine or thirty, it was all the same; it was all in front of her.

He drove into his parking garage looking vaguely for a homeless couple that sometimes set up housekeeping on a cardboard mat near his building. Once, he had given them a hundred-dollar bill. If they were there tonight he would give them every fucking dime in his pocket. They would be suspicious, then shocked, then grateful, the way they were before. Perspective would be his. His blessings would line themselves up like obedient children, and be counted. But the couple and their cardboard lodgings were not there tonight. It was freezing and they had probably had the sense to go to a shelter.

He walked past his doorman and into his building, thinking that there was a time only a few years ago when he was on top of the world. Business boomed. Money poured in in sums so huge he had to close the door to his office and laugh. He was an asshole, but what the hell, everything he did simply went right. His shit was candy. Then, his only regret in life was that he was not a better athlete. It seemed absurd now, but he would have given anything to have been a faster, more graceful runner, more fluid in his movements, lighter in his way of doing things. He was big and built strong, but his body had a clumsiness to it, and he felt terminally earthbound. He had organized his own softball team though, and had manned it with young, wiry, athletic guys: Dominican superintendents from his rentals, construction workers from his high-rise projects, agile young busboys from his restaurants. He had carefully assembled the most brilliant team in the league, and he had taken the whole thing far more seriously than he let on. "They have to let me play," he would joke, "I own the team."

He stepped into the elevator thinking of the day they'd won the league championship. It was a day he had managed to triumph over everything; the laws of gravity had freed him that day and he had flown around the bases, victorious, even over his own clumsy body.

The elevator doors shut. He pushed the button for the penthouse and let his body sink against the carpeted wall.

He closed his eyes.

He was drunk alright, as drunk as he and Faith had both been that night after his team had won the game. He and his uniform were covered with dirt from the softball field, but Faith didn't care. She pressed her body up against his. They kissed deeply. She tasted like fruit, like the Sangria they'd been drinking with the team. It was in this elevator and it was moving, going up, up, and up, when Faith got down on her knees in front of him, unzipped the zipper of his uniform, and took his hard penis in her mouth.

Her hair. He reached out to touch her hair.

Man, you're flying, he had thought. And there was no limit to the pleasure of it. There was no limit to how high or how far a man like him could go.

A CERTAIN NIGHT VIEW

James stood in the underground parking lot looking for his car. His girlfriend, Kayko, had driven it last, and since they were not speaking, he could not very well ask her where she had parked it.

There, he spotted it, one of several absurdly clean, black Porsche Carreras, but he remained still, trying to catch his breath. His asthma was contracting his lungs and all he could get were shallow little bites of oxygen. It was the L.A. air that had brought the asthma on in the first place—"We like to *see* the air we breathe," joked his doctor, but the fight with Kayko had ticked it off. He'd tried to explain to her that he had to attend tonight's party, that it was being given by one of the head partners at his firm, that it was politically uncool not to show, but she wailed, literally, her voice as wounded as though he were driving a knife right into her, "You don't want to be with me. You don't love me." Where was this coming from? It was just a party, and she was *invited*. But nothing he could do would comfort her, and while she'd wail, hurling a telephone across the room and kicking her foot through the flimsy kitchen wall, he'd stand there mute and tense, stunned.

He pulled the inhaler from his jacket pocket and

sucked its contents into his lungs. He held his breath and then exhaled. Then he took his first deep and satisfying breath in minutes. To breathe! He walked to his car trying to shake off the feeling that one day he would finally suffocate.

He got into his car, which always struck him as a model toy scaled up to human size, and pulled out of the parking garage. He drove west on Pico, past the Twentieth Century Fox Studios and into Westwood to pick up his friend Fuller. The payments on the car were wiping him out, and half the time he was terrified to drive the thing for fear that he'd be badly sideswiped or worse. But those worries aside he had to admit how much he loved the car. He'd bought it thinking it would make Kayko happy, but really, he had wanted it, too. If your car said who you were in L.A., then this was who he was going to be. He was amazed at how simple it was. You didn't have to drag around the baggage of your lifetime in L.A., you got to choose who you were, and nobody called you a fraud.

The L.A. offer had beckoned with all the allure of the Gold Rush itself. East Coast law firms could not send their young lawyers out to L.A. fast enough, and James had come hopefully, willingly, to be part of his firm's satellite office ready to handle the expected influx of Pacific Rim business. "Come out for a year," they'd said. "See how you like it," they'd said, dangling the offer in front of him like the keys to someone else's charmed life. Go West, young man. Go West.

And so he had come, at first leaving Kayko at home in Philadelphia, and then sending for her when he'd found himself lonelier than he'd expected. He'd had a crush on Kayko since the eighth grade, and so, when he'd met up with her at a gallery in Philly, and when, there she was, between New York and Rome, between husbands and boyfriends, kind of offering herself, he'd begun an affair with her, inconveniently, recklessly, in the strange, unrooted weeks that preceded his move to L.A.

As a child, Kayko's brothers had been James's closest friends. To his surprise, it was they who chose him, focusing the beam of their attention on him with an irresistible, flattering intensity. He was always over at their house, a privileged witness to their cool indifference as they rocked academic, conservative Bryn Mawr, Pennsylvania.

Their controversial pet pig (in violation of some ordinance or other), plus a number of antique Cadillacs and unfinished metal sculptures parked permanently on their front lawn, inspired a perpetual movement to kick the Takihiro family out of town. Pigs and junk were fixed upon as reason enough to expel them, though clearly there were deeper, less civic-minded reasons for wishing to see them brought down. The town resented the Takihiros' Japanese patriarch, a handsome white-haired artist of talent and some renown, who was rumored to have fathered the children of several of his models in New York and Philadelphia. He was self-absorbed, moody, and arrogant; not at all neighborly. And always unemployed. Who knows what they lived on as the mother's inheritance ran low, while the kids ran wild. James had been fascinated by the depths of feeling the Takihiros inspired in others, such fear, anger, and jealousy. Those who were not at war with the Takihiros were desperate to belong to them. And as a child James had been excited by what it meant to be both reviled and admired—the glamour of infamy. Kayko was the baby.

But James felt a desperation in her love for him that made his insides feel scraped raw. The more she fixed the Takihiro beam upon him, willing him never to abandon her the way she felt her philandering father had, the more he wanted out of its glare.

His friend Fuller was waiting for him on the curb, his hands thrust into his pockets in an elegant, nonchalant pose. He was so tall and thin that he looked precarious standing there, as though he might bend if a strong wind came along. Fuller was a dresser, and being loyal to his East Coast roots he maintained his post-preppy-but-with-flair look in the face, he said, of untold tackiness. The pressure out here to wear white was enormous, and steadfastly, Fuller never succumbed. White was for tennis only, he'd say. Fuller had fashion rules to live by. He also had what amounted to an ironing fetish, and insisted on washing and ironing all of his own shirts. It took hours each week, but Fuller claimed the act of it calmed him in a drug-free kind of way. Also, because of various past laundering injustices, and there had been *a lot* of them, Fuller did not trust the cleaners.

"Hey, loser," Fuller said, bending way down to open the car door. Of course he was dressed impeccably in a chocolate-brown jacket, plum-colored polo shirt, and baggy trousers. He wore his loafers without socks, a look, he insisted, that was European in origin, not one that L.A. could lay any claim to, and therefore okay to do. "Jesus," he said, trying to find a way to fold his very long legs into the passenger's side of the car. "Hey, tasty tie."

"Thanks," James said. He could not help feeling pleased. A compliment from Fuller meant something, and not just to him. Everyone at the firm, from secretaries to partners, basked in a compliment from Fuller, the self-appointed arbiter of taste with the mysterious power to convince others of his authority—an enviable trait in a lawyer, and precocious, too. He was only twenty-six, two years younger than James.

"I thought Kayko was coming," Fuller said, "or is it a touchy subject at the moment?"

"It's a touchy subject at the moment," James said.

"Consider the subject dropped, son," Fuller said. James fingered the silk tie in this season's "vineyard inspired" shades, a gift from the style-savvy Kayko who had been educating James in a number of areas. For instance, who would have guessed the importance of small, delicate flowers in one's salad? And it was Kayko who told him that his looks and his height gave him an edge in life, which made him feel an uncomfortable mixture of pride and intense guilt. These lessons of Kayko's had not been available to him in a childhood that now seemed shaped by the things he had been denied by his well-meaning but militantly unmaterialistic parents: TV, junk food, cool clothes, cars. *Cars*. Fast, expensive cars. He drove, loving the way the car gripped the road.

"Great pickup," Fuller said.

"Want to drive it?" said James.

"No thanks," said Fuller.

"Oh, yeah, I forgot, real New Yorkers don't drive," said James.

"What I wouldn't give for a checkered cab. That's a beautiful car." Fuller hated L.A. and was filled with indignant anecdotes meant to illustrate the righteousness of his position.

"Okay, so I walk into this bookstore on Sunset," Fuller began, "and I ask this babe with fun hair who's sitting behind the counter, wearing all white of course, if they have a copy of *Answered Prayers* and she says, 'Try Religion.' Can you take it, 'Try Religion'? I mean, in New York . . ."

"Here it comes," said James.

"That is right, son. Here it comes," Fuller said, gearing up for a tirade. "In New York would the girl in the bookstore tell me to 'Try Religion'?"

"Of course not," said James.

"Of course not," said Fuller. "In New York the girl in the bookstore would be this incredibly smart Barnard coed—I love that word 'coed'—or she'd be a struggling writer taking workshops at the New School. She'd be a wealth of information on culture in all of its many forms," Fuller said with a flourish of a hand gesture too large for the confines of the car.

"Not everyone here is a moron," said James. James had his own beefs about L.A., like the asthma he'd developed, and how impossible he'd found it to meet people, though generally his objections did not have the cache of snobbism. Besides, there was a certain night view of the city from the Hollywood Hills that he'd seen on TV when Los Angeles had hosted the Olympics in '84. He'd been able to find that view and see for himself how by night the city shimmered. That view seemed a measure of how far he'd come and how far it was possible for him to go.

"Oh, come on," Fuller said. "I mean, in New York even the bums on the street know what's playing at the Met."

"Okay, okay," said James. Fuller made him laugh, and the sound of his own laughter surprised him and made him miss an old sense of himself as someone light-hearted. Suddenly he felt like having a good time tonight. Maybe having more than a few martinis. Maybe having some of the fun, the adventure, the glamour he'd been promised. Maybe flirting with someone in a tight black dress, a girl with fluffy blond hair and mirrored sunglasses that wouldn't let you see her eyes. Tonight he didn't feel like being responsible for what you could see in a woman's eyes.

"Oh, I'm glad you think it's funny," Fuller said, laughing himself now, too. "I'm glad to see that living in a cultural wasteland, a fucking void, is amusing to you."

James kept laughing, enjoying the feeling it gave his body, like stretching your unflexed muscles after a long ride in a car. He drove a little faster.

"Hey, loser, you're not thinking of staying out here, are you?" Fuller asked.

James shrugged. "I like it here," he said. He only had a few more weeks to decide what to do, while Fuller, who'd arrived after James, would have to suffer, loudly, for another six months.

"When my day comes," Fuller said, "I'm going to be packed and on that plane so fast your fucking head will spin. I keep having fantasies about what I'll do my first day back in New York. I imagine I'll be moved to lie down right in the middle of Broadway, in front of Zabar's, and weep with joy."

James had a pang of envy for Fuller who knew so clearly where his happiness lay.

"Look, loser, I wouldn't stay if I were you," Fuller said. "Being here is like waking up on someone's sofa the day after the party."

Fuller had a point. A partner in their department had left the firm and taken their biggest client with him. So now, instead of working with a kind of zealous momentum for the Japanese manufacturer whose cars rolled over and smashed (a "roof integrity problem" they called it), they were sitting around doing busy work for some American company whose cases involved a blatant failure to install air bags. Now, he and Fuller wrote memos that no one would ever read, for cases that would never see the light of the courtroom.

"Look," said Fuller, "you want to sit around and play cards all day?"

James laughed. He had that very day been playing solitaire for hours at his desk, until he'd been beckoned into an office down the hall where Fuller had all the associates embroiled in a heated conversation about whether or not they would ever wear a knockoff. James had not been exactly sure what was meant by a "knock-off," but that was not a problem for Fuller, who was there to explain such things, without judgment, to those who were eager to learn.

"We've beamed down in Colonial Williamsburg," said James.

They had reached Hancock Park and the home of the firm's most senior L.A. partner, William Cobb III, who went by the upbeat and decidedly uncharacteristic nickname, Trip. Trip was not an upbeat guy. Well, that was as far as anybody knew Trip, that is. It was difficult to tell exactly what kind of a guy he was beyond his wing-tipped shoes, his Brooks Brothers' suits, and his paper-white shirts, since James and Fuller hardly ever saw him. They estimated that in the past year, Trip had spent about one hundred eighty days out of the state traveling on behalf of the firm. Trip was polite and reserved in public, but could rake someone over the coals privately. He particularly disliked Fuller whom he had seriously reprimanded on account of Fuller's "horrid attitude."

Fuller popped the car door.

"Look, a front yard. It's like someone just plopped it down here," he said. "See, even the partners don't want to be here. They uproot their socially connected wives, they yank their children out of school, and then they travel all the time. The guy is on his fourth marriage and he wonders why." Fuller was ready, since the "horrid attitude" balling out, to find even more fault with the whole situation.

"No swimming pools. No movie stars," said James as they walked up the brick path together.

"No palm trees. No cacti," said Fuller, operating the large brass knocker.

A Mexican maid in a starched gray uniform ushered them into the living room. She was a middle-aged woman with ashen skin, a ponytail too young for her age, and a missing tooth. James felt a twinge of guilt as he thought of his mother, who had worked tirelessly to help El Salvadoran refugees, a whole family of which was now living in his old bedroom back in Bryn Mawr. When she had come to L.A. for a conference on El Salvador, he'd taken her to Kayko's favorite place, an elegant airy bistro, where she'd thought the prices were insane and the flowers on the salad were silly. She wouldn't understand a party like this, the expense of it, the wasted *funds*.

"I hope you realize this party is in full swing," Fuller said. They stood in the living room amid a depressing array of people from work who were all chatting ineptly in low voices. He and Fuller lifted wineglasses and toothpick-skewered shrimp from the silver trays being passed around. This was hardly the type of affair to cut loose at. There were no martinis to get drunk on, and no girls with fluffy blond hair wearing tight black dresses and mirrored glasses that wouldn't let you see their eyes. An actual Christmas tree stood in the corner decorated tastefully with white fairy lights and wooden, Victorian-looking ornaments. Christmas. Who could think of Christmas when the temperature stayed at seventy degrees and the sun warmed your face as you drove fast down Highway 1?

Howie Friedman, another junior associate, sidled up to Fuller and James.

"Hey y'all," he said. Howie was a Southern Jew, dark and Semitic-looking with the liltingly soft vocal mannerisms of his native Georgia. Priscilla Clark appeared beside him. She was in charge of Trip's silver pen, the Christmas gift from everyone in Products Liability.

"I've got it right here in my bag," she said, patting the side of her purse. She was a tall, slim, lockjawed woman who was followed everywhere by a persistent rumor that at the age of thirty-six she was still a virgin. At the office she kept a teddy bear beside her in her chair. James noticed that Fuller lit up whenever Priscilla came around. He claimed to have a morbid fascination with her alleged virginity and said that he prayed the topic would somehow come up for discussion. He did wicked impressions of her lockjawed speech, but James suspected that Fuller actually liked Priscilla, that he secretly had a flicker of a thing for her.

"I think we should present Trip with his gift over coffee and dessert. What do you guys think?" Priscilla said.

"What's this?" Fuller said, pointing to the wrapped package sticking out of Howie Friedman's jacket pocket.

"If you must know," he answered Fuller in his lilting voice, "I've bought Trip a set of small silver frames. For his children's pictures."

"Oh, excuse me," Fuller said, "I think I see shit on your nose there, Friedman."

"Now come on," said Priscilla. "If Howie wants to get his own gift, I think we should all respect that."

James was beginning to feel a little high from the wine on an empty stomach. He began to laugh.

"Y'all are so ignorant," Howie Friedman said. He then turned and walked away, making no secret of the huff he was in.

"You know he has a medical degree, don't you?" Fuller said. "Ever wonder why he doesn't use it?"

"I think he killed someone on the operating table," said James.

"You guys . . ." Priscilla said as the two of them

nudged her into the unenviable role of "the mature one." Priscilla was a good sport.

"James, where's Kayko?" she asked.

"Sick," he said.

"That's a shame. I hope she's feeling better soon," Priscilla said warmly.

"Thanks," James said. It had dawned on him lately that everybody knew that his relationship with Kayko was in shambles. He heard tremendous amounts of gossip about everyone else at the firm, why should he be exempt from it? He heard himself screaming at Kayko on the phone from his office, "Well, what am I supposed to do about it, Kayko? You have to improve your own life. I can't fix everything for you." Of course everyone on his floor had heard him. Of course they all knew. Suddenly James didn't care about who knew what. He lifted another glass of wine from the floating silver tray.

"You're a nice person, Priscilla," he found himself saying.

Priscilla looked surprised. He'd meant she was nice to pretend with him that Kayko was sick.

"And she's kind to teddy bears, too," said Fuller.

"I know you guys are putting me on," she said.

Trip's wife appeared in the doorway to the dining room. He and Fuller had been right about all of Trip's attempts to re-create his East Coast habitat, but they'd been wrong to imagine a wife dressed in khakis and espadrilles. She was L.A. all the way, in her pale blue beaded dress. James was struck by the brilliant blue of her eyes. Their sapphire color sparkled, and it struck James that her eyes, their color, were the only aspect of her face that had been part of her original beauty. She'd had it all done. What could be lifted, tucked, or reconstructed had been, and now she looked neither old nor young, plain nor pretty. She just looked expensive. Her face had a somewhat pained look that James took to mean, *I'm trying.* She probably hadn't realized the level of boredom she was in for when she'd agreed to be the wife of a head partner. "Shall we all . . ." she said, inviting her guests into the dining room.

Trip and his wife sat at the head of the horseshoe-shaped table looking like dinner guests who had not been introduced to one another. Above them hung an ornate chandelier from which James noticed two missing bulbs. A bland poached salmon and some overcooked vegetables were being served by the firm's catering crew. He recognized the waiters from the firm's dining room and glanced across the table at Fuller who shook his head and rolled his eyes, discreetly, for James's benefit.

As the waiters began to clear away the dinner plates, Trip wiped the corners of his mouth with a stiff white napkin and said, "Excuse me." James watched his boss rise from the table and disappear through a side door.

The waiters came around with coffee and laid dessert plates in front of each guest.

"Where's Trip?" asked Priscilla. It was her moment to present the gift.

"I'm sure he'll be right back," said the wife. But she did not look sure at all.

"Excuse me," she said, and disappeared through the same side door that had swallowed her husband.

"He's going to Cleveland in the morning, maybe he has to pack," Howie Friedman suggested.

"I'm surprised you're not up there packing for him," Fuller said.

Everybody laughed, and for a moment the mood was giddy, as though Mom and Dad had left the kids alone in the house, but when Trip's wife returned her perfect face looked stricken.

"He's gone," she said. "Gone to Cleveland. I'm sorry." She lowered herself slowly into her chair. "Let's just go ahead with dessert," she said quietly.

The wife's show of bravery was disheartening. James presumed that everyone would have felt a lot better if she had just run sobbing from the room. People began scraping the rubbery cherry topping from the cheesecake. James waved away the coffee and took another sip of his wine.

Mercifully, the strained conversation was interrupted by the high-pitched whine of a Porsche car alarm going off outside. James, Howie Friedman, and several others excused themselves to see whose car was shrieking. Sometimes nothing but a breeze blowing by could tick off these car alarms. They were touchy, sensitive creatures.

The car alarm was James's and the others went back inside.

James opened his car door, sat down in the driver's seat, and turned the thing off. He knew he should go back inside and face whatever it was that had to be faced, but while the others choked down cheesecake with a mettle they never could have guessed the job would demand of them, James sat with the door open, thinking about his very clean car.

Last week, on the day before payday, he'd been down to his last ten bucks, and he knew he could either eat lunch or get the car cleaned. Back home in Philadelphia such quandaries as eat-or-drive-a-clean-car would never have even presented themselves. He simply would have eaten, and then driven around in his dust-covered VW Rabbit, oblivious to any unwritten rules about such things. But out here in L.A. he was sure that people really did think less of you if your car was not clean, and you found yourself shifting around the way you thought about things in order to abide by the laws of wonderland.

He felt an unexpected pang of homesickness for the town he'd grown up in. He just wanted some snow crunching underneath his feet. It was, after all, ten days before Christmas. He thought of his father. James had seen him one snowy morning standing on the platform, waiting for the commuter train that would take him into Philly where he was a social worker. There he stood in his ill-fitting clothes, bidding his well-dressed neighbors good morning. They nodded and passed him and huddled together in tight little groups that excluded his father. His family was unpopular, he realized as he observed his father standing alone on the platform. They were too earnest and impassioned. They didn't drink or understand how to socialize. His father spent his free time over in Chester building houses for the homeless. He never mowed the lawn. He never, ever washed the car.

"Hey, loser." It was Fuller coming down the path.

James got out of the car and slowly rose to his feet. "I think I'm a little drunk, thank God," he said.

"Boy are you lucky, son," Fuller said, seating himself on a wrought-iron lawn chair. "Watch this," he said. He thrust his long arms in front of him and lunged forward like the crash test dummy they'd watched over and over in a film about driver's side air bags. Fuller's gangly body fell between his knees and then lurched backward in perfect, horrifying slow motion. "We slow the film waaay down," he announced, as the film's wooden narrator had, "so we can see exactly *what* is hitting the body *where*." Once again he flung his body into the invisible crash. He'd captured it, the mechanical obedience to the laws of physics—the blow, the impact, the stunned rebound.

Normally James would have laughed like crazy, as he always did at Fuller's impressions, like the one Fuller did around the office of a girl in a tie-dyed T-shirt, dancing stoned at a Grateful Dead concert (that one had brought on near fatal conniptions). With the gift of his exaggerated limbs, Fuller was able to capture the spirit—no, the *truth*—of the girl in the tie-dyed T-shirt, as he now captured the truth of the crash test dummy. But James found he was not really laughing, just staring, and suddenly he felt older than Fuller, less able to throw himself into things, to inhabit the spirit of anyone but himself.

James turned and began to walk up the path toward the house, and without an audience, Fuller lost the spirit too, and straightened up and followed.

"Let's go back to my place and crack open a decent bottle of scotch," Fuller said. "I'm not nearly as drunk as I could be."

"Yeah, okay," James said.

To James's surprise, Fuller rested a hand on James's shoulder, a gesture that moved him unexpectedly.

Inside, Priscilla and Howie gave James a concerned, where-were-you kind of look. "I had to fix my car alarm so it wouldn't go off again," he lied; he had no idea how to fix anything.

He wandered around looking for Trip's wife and opening the kitchen door, he saw her, alone at the sink, her head bowed over a pile of dirty dishes. She looked up, startled, and James knew it was too late to just turn around and walk back out. Her deep blue eyes looked teary. "Oh," she said, just "Oh."

"I have to leave," he said awkwardly. "I just wanted to thank you for a lovely dinner."

"Well, you boys are very charming," she said. The sadness in her eyes filled him with dread. Like Kayko's eyes. He didn't love Kayko, and she knew.

"Great party," he said. He backed out of the kitchen door and walked through the dining room, again noticing the missing bulbs in the chandelier, like no one really lived here, like no one noticed or cared. He felt his breathing getting tight.

"Let's get the fuck out of here," he said, grabbing Fuller's arm.

"Priscilla, won't you join us in a fine bottle of scotch," Fuller said as James yanked him along. "You can sit on my lap."

"You guys . . ." she said.

James and Fuller climbed into the car and drove west on Wilshire. "Jesus Christ," said Fuller, which pretty well summed it up, though they continued to deconstruct the party—those missing lightbulbs, how tacky, cheap really, to use the firm's catering staff. And Trip's wife, the poor woman. Yes, she was a beauty.

A light rain began to fall and they pulled over to fasten the roof onto the car. When they got back into the car James felt damp and soggy and short of breath.

"Hey, man, can I crash on your sofa?" he said.

"That bad?" said Fuller.

"Look." He pointed at the chip in his rimless glasses. "Tonight she took a swing at me."

"No shit," said Fuller. He seemed impressed by the drama of the act.

"No shit," said James.

"Look, son, why don't you just break up with her," said Fuller.

James thought of the way baby hairs grew around her hairline. Tiny little downy hairs, soft and vulnerable-looking. They rimmed her hard, angry face, making her look like a mad little child. He was dying to get away from her.

"I can't do that," said James.

"Why not?"

"For one thing, she doesn't have any money," said James.

The rain turned suddenly hard and splattered down onto the windshield in big pelletlike drops.

"You don't have to change your life for someone just because you lusted after them in junior high," said Fuller.

"She doesn't know people here. She's not a self-sufficient kind of person."

"An honorable man," said Fuller. "How did someone like me get mixed up with someone like you." Fuller frowned as he tried to brush the rain from his jacket. "If this is ruined," he said, "I'll slit my wrists."

The rain had begun to let up by the time they pulled into Fuller's apartment complex.

"This is eighteen-year-old McCallan's," said Fuller, holding up the bottle. "Let's celebrate the fact that it never rains in L.A. And Christmas—merry Christmas. And me and you getting the fuck out of here."

They decided to take the bottle of scotch up to the hot tub on the roof.

The hot tub looked eerie with its underwater flood-lights and the mist that rose as the raindrops continued to fall. They bolted from the sheltered patio into the bubbling tub in their boxer shorts, holding their scotch glasses above the water level.

James let his body feel the intense pleasure of being submerged. The warm water swirled around his back and legs as the rain sprinkled down on his face and hair. Holding his scotch glass high, he dunked his whole body underwater and then came up for air. He took a large sip of his drink and looked out at the city.

There from Fuller's rooftop he could see his favorite view of L.A.'s twinkling lights. It's just the heat that causes things to shimmer, thought James. Pollution, anything in the atmosphere causes lights to twinkle. He'd always felt that everybody knew something he did not, some great secret that made clear how to be admired in the world. The Takihiros knew it, Fuller knew it, all of Los Angeles knew it. But now, looking out on the miles of little barrios, at a bunch of electric lights that shimmered in the polluted air, he was certain that he knew as much or as little as anybody did, and he couldn't remember what he'd thought was so great about the view.

GEOGRAPHY

"If you lived in New York I never would have met you."

You are always telling James this.

"In New York," you say, "a man like you would have been snapped right up."

At this point he will say, "Oh, Faith," and shrug, gracefully, the way he does most everything.

"Go ahead and shrug," you say. "I know what I'm talking about."

Most people's boyfriends are not as handsome as yours. With his soft brown eyes, his square jaw, and his high cheekbones, your boyfriend is more handsome than anyone even needs a boyfriend to be. When girl-friends ask, so, what does James look like? you get to say back, he's just plain handsome, and not handsome in an offbeat or interesting way either, which is how you must invariably describe most good boyfriends, although how would *you* know, never having gone after the *good* boyfriends before?

"Your handsomeness is icing on the handsome cake," you are always telling him. This makes him blush or roll his eyes. A nice touch.

You hurry to meet him for iced coffee at a Center

City deli whose walls are covered with minor celebrities. All those eight by tens, all those glossies, all those B-list stars. You try not to let them, but the glossies make you homesick for New York, for the real thing, for the most ordinary drugstore on Columbus Avenue with signed photos of Barbra Streisand, John Lennon, Woody Allen, Leonard Bernstein, Cher. Here, the wall space is reserved for people like Connie Sellecca, Kim Fields, Hulk Hogan, a number of former Miss Pennsylvanias, and several local piano bar players all named Tommy or Timmy *Toons*. You wonder what could have brought the semifamous here, to this, THE OFFICIAL DELI OF THE PENNSYLVANIA BALLET (the menu says this, you swear, though it's hard to imagine tiny little ballerinas ripping into corn beef on rye). You wonder, could they all have come to Philadelphia because they fell in love, the way you did?

Your boyfriend is sitting, waiting with his glass of iced coffee.

"Sneakers."

"Rabbits."

The pet names. In public. And loudly, too.

The caution of your former life has been thrown to the wind. You have taken a glorious swan dive off a cliff. You are riding on air and you like it. You like being part of one of those couples who hug passionately in the supermarket.

Your boyfriend smiles. The beam of his attention is on you and it casts a glow, a limelight that makes you beautiful. And you thought . . . never mind what you thought. Let's just say that this kind of glow-limelight thing has exceeded your expectations. By a lot.

"You made it," your boyfriend says.

"Of course," you say. The fact that you have been driving around Philadelphia without a driver's license makes him nervous, though not quite nervous enough to try to get you to stop.

You've brought your boyfriend's prescription inhaler with you, his "puffer," he calls it. First it rains, then the sun shines, then it rains again. The weather, its unpredictability, makes his asthma act up.

Your boyfriend takes a puff and holds his breath for ten long seconds. You hold your breath, too, just to be on the safe side.

"Look, Joe Frazier," he says on the breath of the exhale.

You look around.

"On the wall," he says, pointing.

"Oh, yeah."

It's Joe Frazier in his trunks, gloves up.

Now you know things about boxing.

When your boyfriend is not sure what he really wants to do with his life, he gets depressed and goes to work out at a boxing gym owned by Joe Frazier. Joe Frazier calls him, "Lawyer. Hey, Lawyer."

"Ah, ah, ah, ah," your boyfriend makes these sounds as he shadowboxes around the bedroom. "Ah, ah, ah, ah," a cross between a hum and a growl. He makes these sounds as he boxes with the steering wheel, or with your cat who takes an occasional swing back at him. Ah, ah, ah, ah. "It's your mantra," you tell him.

"I had a conversation with Missy today," he tells you. "She called my office."

Missy is your mutual friend back in New York, a painter who is working on a series of bulldogs with real hair and real teeth and ceramic heads that pop right out of the canvas. "Save me your hair," she tells anyone going for a haircut. "And of course if your teeth fall out, I'll take them too," she says. Missy is the one who fixed you and your boyfriend up on a blind date. Missy had a feeling that the two of you should meet. Missy knew things about your future that you did not even suspect.

"Missy," you say. Her name is not without a certain amount of magic to you, but your heart stirs a little too much at the mention of the name Missy, and you find yourself poised for news from New York. Stories from the art world. Important information from the hub of things.

"Her aunt in Connecticut died," your boyfriend

tells you. "And before she died she told Missy that the two most important things to a dying person are love and oxygen."

You take each other's hands.

This is news from farther beyond than you had expected.

You walk your boyfriend back to his office, a well-kept town house with brass railings. He holds you tightly around your waist as you walk.

The drizzle again. You have your umbrella up.

"I miss you today," he says.

"I miss you today," you say.

"You always miss me," he says.

"No, no, today, I miss you even more than usual."

Back in New York you actually had girlfriends who said things like: Men are like dogs and cats; they're nice, and we share the planet with them, but why would you ever want to have a romantic relationship with one?

Some of the older women had had their one precious child. Others knew it was getting too late for even the precious one. Some of them had lovers who were married, and who lived far away, safely out of reach, in places like North Dakota or South Africa. But all of them had gone beyond hoping, beyond bitterness even, beyond love.

You found their dog, cat, same planet proclamations terrifying. You were thirty now and saw how things could go. So easily, too.

Your chiropractor talked about her career. She was a pale but wrinkle-free woman who believed in the sun's damaging rays and wore bright red lipstick, for a little excitement, she said. You could get so much done, she told you, when you stopped worrying about men. She was an original thinker, whose genius you respected. She once got your period to start by rubbing your pubic bone a certain way. She had the touch.

She placed her hands on your back. You were like a cat, leaning into her stroke. Her small hand on your left shoulder blade made you want to cry. You felt bewildered; the pleasure of simply being touched was not yet lost on you. There, facedown on the chiropractic table, you became afraid of turning into a cat lady, one of those women who lives alone in a studio apartment on the Upper West Side with as many cats as she can afford to feed. The whole place reeks of cat piss, but the cat lady no longer notices the smell. She's lost her sense of it.

"Maybe I'll get another cat," you said into the face-shaped identation of the chiropractor's table.

"Now there's an idea," she said. "A girl can never have too many cats."

On a given day in Philadelphia you may take your boyfriend's dog for a walk. You may take him for two walks. Even three.

You try to get the hang of the neighborhood. Rehabilitated, they call it—it is filled with gutted factories waiting to be made into chic dwelling spaces for pioneers of fashionable living. But Philadelphia is a dying city, the newspapers say, and so, what was supposed to be up-and-coming sits like a ghost town. You can almost see the tumbleweeds blowing down the empty streets.

"Always walk below Girard Street, never above it," James has warned you. You don't even want to know what goes on above Girard Street, he tells you. Above Girard Street lies trouble, lies danger even, lies despair.

You walk up Fourth, *below Girard Street,* passing little brick row houses flying their American flags, displaying their yellow ribbons. You wait for the neighborhood to take shape, but with its motley mix of blue-collar families, young professionals, and eyebrow-pierced film buffs who work at the video store, it never does.

You walk past a church with a curlicue sign that says IGLASIA CHRISTIANA MISSIONERA. Outside on the sidewalk an old woman wearing beat-up white nurse's shoes and a sequined hat sits, legs splayed, in a faded plastic lawn chair, the fabric of her housedress pulled tautly between her knees like the canvas on a trampoline.

"Imelda Marcos came for Easter services last year," she tells you. Her voice is a whiskey-coated growl.

"That's interesting," you say, unsure if she means this unsolicited information to be a selling point of the neighborhood or not. Is it even true? You muster a vague smile as you yank the dog away from the woman's lap and walk.

You walk but you cannot locate the center of things. Business signs say things like LIBERTIES GLASS AND MIRROR CO. or NORTHERN AUTO DETAILING. You do not need auto detailing. You need a place to have coffee and a bagel. You need a bookstore, a newsstand, a shop that carries your photography and art supplies, a little Korean market devoted to the freshest fruits and vegetables. You need boutiques full of dazzling shoes you could never afford. You need a hole in the wall where you can get a manicure cheap, and without an appointment. You need to know that if you really wanted to you could walk around the corner and spend eight dollars on a single jar of jam. You need a *New York Post*, its lurid headlines announcing what people really think, not what they should. Back in New York your massage therapist tells you why satire doesn't work in film; your hairdresser defines the difference between pornography and art. You long for them.

On your way back home you pass the lady in the sequined hat again. Hot rays of sun hit the hat's mirrored beads and ricochet back out into the sky. There is too much happening on that hat.

"That dog is cryin'," the lady says.

You look. The dog does have a sad, droopy-eyed face. He is wrinkled all over, what you would call "a sight."

"He is not crying," you say. You move away, slowly, backward down the street, aware of the beaded hat's power to mesmerize.

The temperature rises.

When the two of you get home you are both hot and exhausted. The dog gets a bowl of water outside in the little backyard. Your boyfriend has grown a city garden out here. On Saturdays he tends to his tomatoes in his boxer shorts, the ones with the giant ants printed all over them. You love to watch his back muscles as he pulls up weeds and flings them into the weed pile. You pat the dog's wrinkly head. You've overheard your boyfriend talking to the dog, calling him son. How can you not love a man who calls his dog son?

On a given day in Philadelphia your boyfriend may bring home fresh fish and cook it on the grill. You make the salad and whip up a honey mustard vinaigrette with the mango champagne vinegar you brought from New York. You eat by candlelight outside in the backyard on a card table covered with a white tablecloth.

One reason you like your boyfriend so much is that he's talkative and gossipy. He can't wait to tell you things. A partner at his firm is on the verge of a nervous breakdown. Another partner is on a banana diet. A close friend has an old girlfriend with a broken leg living on his couch. And there is more. He can't find the kind of flip-flops he's looking for, the ones with the cushiony soles. Did I know that his ex-girlfriend's grandfather was in a Japanese internment camp? A temp at the office went to Alaska on a cruise ship and is never coming back. You get all of this, as television talk shows and women's magazines continue to feature a book about how men don't want to talk. You get James, who interrupts the loop in your head. You can actually feel the things he says. They pull you in and hold you close.

You drink a toast. To living together, you agree, grinning.

"Look," he says, "fireflies."

They light up, one here, one there, blinking on and

off like tiny little yellow lights. Like a holiday. Like good fortune itself.

Your boyfriend looks awfully smart in a tan summer suit. In the morning you sit up in bed and watch him tie his tie and comb his wet hair. The room smells of his cologne.

"Look," you say, holding out your hand. In your palm you have several dead fleas.

"My circus," he says.

You find yourself laughing at an inconceivably early hour for laughter.

On a given day in Philadelphia, you may ring up large phone bills talking to your friends in New York. When you told one of your closest friends, Kenneth, that you were moving to Philadelphia for what you called an indeterminate amount of time, he looked stricken. Then he gathered himself. He would visit, he assured you.

"I'll come. I'll get the Wanamaker's charge card," he said brightly, trying to put the best possible face on the situation. Kenneth is like that, a best possible face kind of person.

"Guess what?" he tells you over the phone. You are looking out the kitchen window, watching the dog lie in the flower bed. "I was at Bloomingdale's today and nobody recognized me. It kind of depressed me," he says. Two weeks ago three Clinique-counter skin care experts had known him from the Off-Broadway show he's in. "And without my wig and makeup even," he had marveled.

The whole thing makes you giggle. You have known Kenneth for thirteen years and now he has become a minor celebrity. He is tall and slim and elegant and to your mind has always been a celebrity, if that is someone people fear and admire.

"Joan Rivers came last night," he says. "We had our picture taken with her backstage. It should make the columns, although the press people are idiots," he tells you.

Yes, yes, you are hungry for indignant remarks about press people being idiots.

"*Time* magazine came. Word is they loved it," he says. "So what about you?"

"Some lady tried to do voodoo on me with a sequined hat," you say. "We do not lack for glamour here."

"I'll visit soon," Kenneth promises. "We'll go to Wanamaker's and be evil to the sales help. We'll get our underarms waxed."

"Heaven," you say. Outside the dog shifts in the sun and crushes your pansies.

"I got this great Armani coat at Bloomies," Kenneth says. "I've been eyeing it for months, and today it was marked down from six hundred to two-fifty, not that I have any business spending the two-fifty, but anyway, I grabbed it," he says.

"Good for you," you say. Generally, you are in favor of grabbing the goods.

"Have you met anyone?" you ask.

"Yeah, one guy," he says. "he came to the show but I was real mean to him and then I went running down the street."

"Sounds promising," you say.

"Very," he says.

You sigh. You don't like to picture Kenneth listening to his bootleg Julie Andrews tapes alone, or taking a solo pilgrimage to Austria to see where *The Sound of Music* was filmed, which is exactly what he went and did when Matt, his boyfriend, died.

"But guess what?" Kenneth says, his best-possible-face voice ringing through the telephone. "Wrapped up in my brand-new coat, I look just like Audrey Hepburn in *Funny Face*."

You'd give anything to see him twirling around his apartment in it. Anything.

You have fleas. Somewhere in the house there is an infestation of them, living, breeding, making the most of a good thing: four cats, a dog, and your ankles. First, your boyfriend bombs the house with do-it-yourself grenades. The smell of them gives you a headache of the pull-down-the-shades-get-out-the-ice-pack variety. And still you have fleas. A professional exterminator calling himself Big Pete is brought in. Big Pete has a huge round face, watery blue eyes, and occasional tufts of colorless clown hair. Big Pete hunts down the fleas to the tune of several hundred dollars, and finally the fleas are gone. Theoretically, that is. You'll believe it when you see it. You are from the New York school of bug and rodent control.

"Faith of little faith," says your boyfriend. "How'd you ever get a name like Faith, anyway?"

"Yes, well, just think where I'd be without it," you say.

"Think positive," he says. "Think no fleas."

But the next morning he is calling you from work.

"So I sit down at my desk," he tells you, "and guess what jumps off of me?"

"Well, move away from it," you say, "pretend it don't come from you."

In your darkroom they are at your ankles again, biting around in ring formations so that it looks like you are wearing little pink ankle bracelets.

Big Pete is called back.

"It's an emergency," you say.

"Is it life or death?" he asks.

Love and oxygen?

"It is to those of us with fleas eating at our flesh," you say.

"That's some attitude," he tells you. Big Pete is a tsk-tsker, a head shaker.

"Okay, a crisis then," you say, following him down into the basement.

Again, he wags his big head no.

"Can we agree that it's a situation then? Please," you beg. "It would mean a lot of me if we could at least call it a situation."

↝

"You made it," your boyfriend says.

You have driven into the center of town to meet him for lunch. You drive slowly and with caution. When you see a police car you try to lose it by making the next available turn, whatever it is. Every time you make it someplace without being arrested you consider it a triumph.

"Of course I made it," you say.

Your boyfriend does not think driving without a license is so cute anymore. "I'll get it," you tell him,

"I'll get it." But the truth is, every time you sit down with the manual to brush up on blind spots and blinking yellow lights, you fall into a deep dreamless sleep.

It's hot out but you decide to go to the vegetarian cart by the park at Rittenhouse Square. Your boyfriend is a meat-eater. He likes big juicy steaks with pomme frites and Worcestershire sauce. He likes cheese steaks, hamburgers, hot dogs, and beef kabobs, and rare roast beef on a croissant with mayonnaise. But today, for you, it is the vegetarian cart.

"I like meeting for lunch," your boyfriend says, happily. "I like seeing a nonadversarial face across the tofu meatballs."

You take bites of each other's food and watch people walk by with their brown paper bags and cans of diet Coke.

"You know what I've noticed," says James. "I've noticed that people in Philadelphia don't talk to themselves as much as people in New York do."

"Maybe in Philadelphia," you tell him, "they don't have as much to say."

❦

At twenty minutes to seven your boyfriend flies through the door and begins flinging his clothing around the bedroom. His white button-down shirt lands on your favorite camera.

"Seen my boxing gloves?" he says. He is bad at keeping track of things like boxing gloves.

"Closet," you say. You are lying on the bed watching TV. You have become addicted to this show where people allow themselves to bleed openly on national television.

"You're going to the gym again?" you ask. "You just went this morning."

"I thought I'd go back tonight," he says, stuffing yards of that cotton tape he wraps his hands up with into his bag.

"Why twice in one day?"

"I just thought I'd go again tonight, that's all."

"Twice in one day?" How you hate the sound of your own desperate voice.

"I'm on a roll," he says. "Joe Frazier wants to put me in the ring."

"Fine," you say, marching past the television. A chubby girl in a short tight skirt is telling the story of her blind date. "I baked him a huge broken cookie that said, 'Let's make a connection.' "

Your boyfriend follows you down the stairs and into the kitchen. *Ah, ah, ah, ah.*

"What's wrong?" he says.

"Nothing," you say, "I'll just eat by myself."

"Okay," he says, "I won't go."

"No, go," you say, "I feel like a fishwife."

"What's a fishwife?" he asks.

"A fishwife," you shout, "is a fishwife." You have no idea.

Back in New York, on a night when summer has finally turned to fall, you may wrap a coat around you and take a cab through Central Park. You may be on your way someplace that holds some special promise, or someplace that seems a measure of how far you have come. It may be dusk, and as you look out of the window at the buildings beyond the trees, you may feel your heart open up as wide as it can go.

It can happen like that in New York.

You and the dog sit on the back steps with the porch light on, listening to the whirring sounds of the small paper box factory down the street. You think of something your boyfriend said on the drive down from New York to Philadelphia: "I feel like a pioneer man taking his woman west to the homestead." Then he sang, happily, Carpenters' songs.

The dog lays his big wrinkly head in your lap. All right, maybe the dog is crying.

The anniversary of your first date falls on a Sunday. You had meant to celebrate but the temperature has risen to a record one hundred and one degrees. Your boyfriend's asthma is acting up. His chest rattles as he breathes. You spend most of the day inside, in the air-conditioned bedroom, watching a movie on video in which an improbably muscular undercover police officer from Austria infiltrates a kindergarten classroom in search of clues to somebody or other's whereabouts. Even the bedroom shades can't keep the hot sun from streaming through the window and casting an annoying glare on the TV screen. Neither one of you says a word about the flea that hops from his foot onto yours.

Later you drive to a huge home center hardware store looking for a new air-conditioner filter. To accomplish this task you must go *above Girard Street.*

"Lock your doors," says your boyfriend.

You drive by burned-out buildings, on streets lined with rotting garbage, where hot men, half-dressed, drink from bottles hidden in brown paper bags. You drive for miles until it all looks the same, the men, the garbage, the buildings, and then you come upon a large black woman resting in a chair. Beside her, there on the hot filthy sidewalk, a child with a bright pink hair ribbon splashes in a plastic wading pool. Splashing and splashing, laughing and splashing.

"What's wrong?" James asks, his voice filled with alarm.

You are sobbing into your hands, unable to stop.

On Monday it's too late to cook when your boyfriend arrives home from work. You don't feel like cooking anyway. It's still hot outside, dog-breath-hot, James calls it, and both of you just want air-conditioning, something to eat, and a large iced tea.

At the restaurant, an open, airy, informal kind of place with museum art prints on the walls, the air-conditioning blasts cold enough to give you goose bumps, and people seem giddy with relief. The waitress is very young and tanned, a long tangled braid bounces between her shoulder blades as she walks. She takes your order, telling your boyfriend that she's sorry, but they don't have iced tea.

"How about a root beer?" she says, smiling. She really is pretty, and you try to enjoy her beauty, to appreciate it abstractly and without envy, the way a man would.

She rests her hand on your boyfriend's shoulder.

"So it's root beer then?" she asks.

When she walks away you notice how unfashionably heavy she is, but also how certain she is of her allure. In her white cutoff jeans and her red and white tank top she has the sex appeal of another era, like a 1950s Coca-Cola pinup girl. You wish you had washed your hair today. Really, clean hair would mean a lot right now.

"You know I never say things like this, but I think that waitress likes me," your boyfriend says.

"Really?" you say, taking small bites of swordfish.

"Is something wrong?" he asks.

You realize you must look stricken.

You sit in the car and wait as a blanket of dusk settles over the parking lot. Kenneth never did get his Wanamaker's credit card. A sign, you decide, since he called Wanamaker's credit department to ask where the thing was enough times to be on a first-name basis with someone named Wanda. You watch your boyfriend emerge from the restaurant, worry knitting his brow. *Ah, ah, ah, ah.*

"Faith, what is it?" he asks, sliding into the car beside you.

You can feel huge tears rolling down your cheeks, partly because you are miserable and partly because you can tell by the innocence in his voice that he has no idea why you are upset and was never for an instant a party to the flirting that was going on in the restaurant.

"I'm pathetic," you say. "Was I pathetic in New York?"

"Of course not," he says.

"But you agree I'm pathetic now," you say.

"No, I do not agree," he says. He reaches for your hand the way he does at night, when, he says, he can't sleep without touching you.

"That waitress," you say, "she *should* like you."

"What?" he says.

"And she's so pretty and everything, I wouldn't blame you if you liked her, too."

"Are you kidding? That waitress is nothing."

"Men like nothing."

"Oh, come here," he says, pulling you close.

"Do you know that I haven't taken one picture since I got here? Not one," you say. "I just develop all this old film I took in New York. I hate it here," you say, relieved to have spoken it. "I hate it here."

He rubs the back of your neck—he has such a nice touch—but he says nothing, except for a resigned, "I know."

You sit in the parking lot together and watch as other people's cars pull up beside yours. You look on with envy at people who probably don't have geography on their minds. The sky looks pink and purple. You can see the big orange sun setting behind the ratty-looking buildings in front of you. "We The People," says the plastered signs. A rock band maybe. The two of you are quiet, wondering what to do.

"You know what happened today?" your boyfriend says.

"What?" you ask.

"I tried to tip a delivery boy and he refused to take the money. You want to know why?" James goes on. "Well, I asked him why, and he says, 'I'm delivering for free today because I could use the karma.' I could use the karma, I love that."

You suddenly feel incredibly heavy, so firmly planted on the earth, so ordinary, so like the rest of the world's victims of the inevitable force of gravity. Sometime, a while ago, you, in your glorious swan dive, landed.

"Anyway," he says, leaning forward to rest his forehead on the steering wheel, "I just wanted to tell you about it, that's all."

You touch his hair.

"It made me laugh," he says. "All kinds of things make me think of you."

BACK FROM
THE WORLD

He has decided never to get over her.

He wears his broken heart with a perverse kind of pride, like a medal from a war, a badge of obstinance he pins to himself each day as he goes about his job, and what you would call his life.

It is also a point of reference.

There are flying rats and loping dinosaurs, prostitutes and army men, and birds, always birds, endless pages of small, inky drawings. Sandy's basement room in his parents' house is full of them. And poetry. There is his poetry, which cascades in his mind all day as he performs the tasks of his maintenance job for the small town he grew up in.

He has turned thirty and thirty-one and now thirty-two, and, he feels, has made the transition from troubled youth to local eccentric. He knows his lack of ambition makes people embarrassed. People no longer ask about college or his plans. He has been to the army, to Germany. He has been to the Peace Corps, too. And he has been to New York City, to Columbia University to study ornithology, the science of birds, though everybody knows the real reason he went up there was to be with *her*. He has escaped to all the places a young man can escape to, and he is back again, an expeditionist who failed to make a claim. Back from the world.

There is much to be maintained in this town. More than half of its two hundred acres are parks and woods. It is a national historic landmark, a one-time Methodist campsite whose oddly shaped houses were once summer tents. Now these cottages, expanded over time, added on to in funny bits and pieces are a gingerbread mix of styles: Victorian, Gothic revival, and pure ramshackle. Every so often *The Washington Post* does an article on the town, always calling it "Virginia's anachronism" and "quaint," "a town within a forest" or "a town ignoring time."

He drives the town tractor, mowing its many fields of grass. Summer is almost here. It is the clover making the grass smell so sweet. People wave and he waves back, as though his life, fractured and unwhole, is at least settled for now into this ruined pattern, like an eyesore, someone's architectural mistake that the whole town must simply live with after the bickering dies down.

Today he must cut the dead branches from the large oak tree on Main Street, across from the house where *she* grew up. Grew up so gracefully, he must note.

Her name is Faith. Faith Banning. And as the whole town knows, she is the love of his life, and always was. If only he could have been a scientist like his brother, working for a foundation or a university, he might have been able to keep her, for to his amazement, after years of adolescent longing, he had, as an adult, been able to track her down more or less betweeen boyfriends, and to attract her with his passionate lovemaking and his devotion. With his tenderness. Passionate, devoted lovers were all but extinct in New York City, she said. Tenderness an anachronism. Imagine, she sighed, while he buried his head between her legs. How rare.

But the poetry came back, and he sat in their tiny studio apartment taking it down like dictation while he should have been in class or writing papers or thinking about graduation and getting a real job with the Audubon Society or the Museum of Natural History. How he had let her down. You're nothing but a pothead, she had said. And it was not the remark itself that wounded him so, because, yeah, he'd smoked some dope, but the bitterness with which she said it, and the fact that he had caused a woman to be bitter.

He cuts the dead branches into smaller pieces with an ax, using an old stump as a chopping block. He notes some geese as they fly overhead. Canada Goose, *Branta canadensis,* Audubon plate no. 32. Force of habit. Migrating is a stupid thing to begin with and he notices geese aren't doing it much anymore.

He chops wood into the afternoon, amazed at how quickly the hours pass. Work is work. Work is one foot in front of the other, one labor, one task at a time, and though he does not look forward to it, neither does he fear it. It is his connection to the physical realm, anchoring him to a day-to-day life in which a picnic table must be painted in time for a holiday, leaves must be raked because it is fall, grass must be mowed because it is summer.

A girl named Chatsworth, Cat, speeds by on her bicycle. She waves and he waves. This Cat girl exercises like a demon, racing around town on her ten-speed bike. He'd heard she was anorexic, but she really isn't looking all that skinny anymore. He wonders if she craves food. Is she excited by it, or disgusted? Or is she over it now, her adolescent fling with self-starvation, with death. Is she normal again? Is she hungry?

The words "statutory rape" run though his mind, although he has no idea if so old-fashioned sounding a law even exists in Virginia. Cat is still in high school, he believes, and he has never before been attracted to someone who is still in high school. Well, not since he was still in high school, that is. It's absurd, his attraction to the girl. She isn't pretty. What would he and the Cat girl have in common besides the town itself, which because of its anachronism status is the source of endless chauvinism and snobbery among its residents?

For these past two years, since coming back from the world, his lovers have all been women older than himself, some married to husbands he waves to as they drive off to work in the morning, some divorced, and one widowed by a suicide. And there was one who would allow him to enter her only from behind. I can't face you, she'd said, I can't face myself.

Sandy is not without his vanity and he has been pleased to please these women, to provide them with their fantasy of the sweaty, shirtless groundskeeper, to take the time their husbands wouldn't take, to suck their clean pink toes, one by one. But Cat has made him aware of his age, of the premature gray hair that runs in his family. He is getting fat—cheap, starchy food and too much beer—though he still runs his four to five miles a day.

No, he will not pursue an anorexic high school girl. Her youth and the possibility that her condition makes her vulnerable in love would make him feel like a creep, and so far he is not a creep and would like to keep it that way.

The days pass and he finds himself aware of the time of day. The Cat girl gets out of school at three o'clock in the afternoon. She is home by three-thirty; on her bike by three forty-five. He waves and she waves. That is all.

How he wishes it were a mirage, the documentary film crew that follows him about the town. But for once this particular irritating vision is quite real. These not-for-profit do-gooders have been given a grant to do a film about the town for public television, and they are up early most mornings, following him in their pickup truck, recording the sound of his tractor with a microphone.

"Hey, how's it going?" yells a guy with a beard.

But he will not speak. He will allow others to speak for him. Tell his tale. The boy who grew up in this town but could never quite make his way in the world outside it. Keeper of the grounds. The one and only employee of the town. He will let others characterize him. Perhaps they will think he is mute. An anachronistic local eccentric, he. A bird-watcher. Or perhaps he will speak a poem and they will have all the faded gentility they need, and will pack up and go.

"I say, man, how's it going? Have you lived in the town for long?"

Sandy guns the tractor's motor and speeds ahead. An old crank. A young, old crank.

He makes it to the lake, where, for now anyway, he has managed to ditch the film crew. He dismounts his tractor, which he can't help thinking of as "trusty," and goes to unlock the shed where the algae net is kept. Summer is nearly here, and the lake must be readied for tireless suntanned children and their mothers bearing beach towels and sandwiches. He stands on the dock with a net and tries to fish the thin film of algae out of the water.

The lake is man-made and was dug out from a natural spring about seventy-five years ago. It won't clean itself. It is his job to clean it, and he is thankful for the labor it takes.

He knows the shoreline of this lake, its curve, where the land will swell or dip beneath his next step, as well as he knows anything. The shoreline of this lake, he thinks, my area of expertise, the only thing I really know.

Perhaps his net will come upon the snapping turtle, which is really more than one snapping turtle, maybe as many as five or six, and "it" has never, as he has always heard people say, grabbed on to someone's foot and refused to let go. But he knows how a legend can persist, despite the truth.

He hears the splattering sound of tires treading over gravel and looks up to see the Cat girl peddling down the path, coming toward him at top speed.

"Just warning you," she calls out, "the film crew is coming."

Sandy drops his net and runs for the tractor. He hops on and drives behind a thick wall of cattails. He turns off the engine, climbs down from the tractor, leans against the wheel, and waits. The Cat girl reappears through the long reeds, pushing her bicycle through the marsh.

"What is the big whoop over small towns?" she asks, leaning her bicycle up against the tractor. "Mention small towns and everybody goes ape shit, whipping out the checkbooks. What do they think they're going to find here, family values? What about the seedy underbelly? How about some grant money for the seedy underbelly? I personally object to the way NEA grant money is being handled by the fascists."

Ape shit? Fascists? Underbellies? Sandy has never really heard the Cat girl speak. Until this moment behind the cattails she has been not much more than another kid growing up in this town, a kid his sister or Faith probably baby-sat for. He watches as she pushes her short brown hair away from her eyes and loosens the blue bandanna she has twisted around her neck.

"Do you think they want to come over to my house and watch my mother hover over me while I choke down solid food?"

She is quite astonishing, he decides. With freckles. Her feet and hands are very large. She wears silver hoops in her ears and a thin, knotted band of leather around her ankle.

He makes a gesture with his fingers toward her lips.

"Shhh," he murmurs.

He hears the film crew coming with their cameras and their microphones and their wobbly silver reflecting sphere, which they hold up to capture the light. *They* of the khaki shorts are coming down the path, huffing and puffing on foot because he has locked the outer gate against their vehicle.

He and Cat are quiet enough so that he is privy to the lovely sound of her breathing. He dares to look at her face, and she dares, daring girl, to look back. Her eyes are a deep brown and far apart, and there is something uneven about them, something defiant in their lack of uniformity, as though her face itself issues forth a challenge to symmetry, to the order of things.

"You remind me of a comic book character called She-Rah, He-Man's twin sister," he whispers. "As I recall, She-Rah could breathe under water."

"Special powers huh?" she says, narrowing her eyes.

"I'd say so," he says, still whispering.

"I like that," she says, "I'm a feminist."

"Ah," he says, "a feminist."

"Yes," she says, "and that is why I cannot get along with high school boys. They think I'm a lesbian."

"Is that so?" he says, mightily intrigued.

"They are so immature," she whispers.

"Lowest form of life in the cosmos," he says. "Take it from one who knows."

Voices can be heard beyond the cattails, and he and Cat are both quiet a moment listening for the film crew. They are out there, wondering, no doubt, what has happened to their prey.

"Let me ask you this," she says in a hushed voice. "Why do you stay here when you're not stuck here to rot like I am, when you can go anywhere?"

"You don't look rotten," he says.

"The rot is on the inside," she says.

"I know what you mean," he says. "How old are you, anyway?"

"Oh, please," she says. "How old are you?"

"Want to see something?" he asks her.

He parts a row of cattails. Behind the tall reeds black and yellow spiders the size of silver dollars have their webs spinning everywhere, like shiny, loosely woven lace, shivering and sparkling in the sun.

"Jesus," she says.

"May I call you?" he asks.

"Of course not," she says. "I'll meet you somewhere."

Sandy can hardly subject a lover of his to a basement room filled with dank artifacts and collected bottles from the woods, musty stacks of books, and scattered pages of poetry and drawings.

He has been entrusted with the key to the McKibbys' house, which he is watching for its owners while
they are in England for a year of academic fellowship.
He sits nervously on the McKibbys' double bed, the
double bed of those naive and guileless McKibbys who
have no idea that their house will be used for illicit sex,
for a rendezvous with a teenaged recovering anorexic
who refuses to disclose her chronological age. He is
wondering exactly how to go about seducing a high
school girl when he hears her barging noisily up the
stairs. She appears in the doorway, her ten-speed bike
hoisted above her shoulder.

"I can't leave it outside," she says, "someone might
see it."

"Of course," he says. He rises quickly to take the
bike off her hands, but she beats him to it, setting the
thing down and leaning it gently against an antique bureau.

Cat stands there for a moment looking too girlish
in her bike shorts and sneakers, her short brown hair
cropped off in a blunt haircut. He stands there, too,
awkwardly, he knows, unsure of what to do next. He
would like to kiss the supple nape of her long neck.

"If you're wondering if I'm a virgin, I'm not," she
says.

"Oh, okay," he says, nodding his head. Why hadn't

he been wondering about it? She could have been a virgin. Creep, perv, statutory rapist, he thinks.

She moves toward him and he touches her soft brown hair. Don't go through with it, he tells himself, but she is in his arms now. He cups her small chin in his hand and kisses her more deeply than he had meant to, and than he had imagined he would. As he leads her toward the McKibbys' double bed he notices how easy it is to cross over the lines you have drawn for yourself, how very easy, like falling, like slow motion. Once you have done it.

Later in the evening he sits at his desk in his musty basement cell and records the poetry that came to him during the day. His parents, retired teachers, spend most of their time now at their cabin in the Blue Ridge Mountains. But still, he confines himself to his cave in the basement, where the dark and the damp will occasionally attract a miraculous little frog, or an interesting species of spider.

The geese find their way into a poem, flying oddly, syncopated, outside their usual V formation. Circling, he finds the geese of his poem are circling for a land. And Cat, whose smell is still on him. An image of her long swan's neck comes to him and forms itself nicely into couplets. But he doesn't jot this one down. Just lets it flow. He thinks of her eyes, brown and uneven, which inspire no poetry at all, but glare and squint with their realist's view of the world.

He remembers when he finally showed Faith a handful of the many poems inspired by her, years' worth. You're making me up, she told him. This isn't me. I'm not Venus. But by then she was annoyed with him. By then he'd made her weary. Her acting career was going nowhere, she said. She was recording pornographic voice-overs, which, she said, were destroying enough of her brain cells to notice. Sandy found the phone sex sexy in the corny, obvious kind of way that makes men hot, and that women are contemptuous of. But all of it made Faith scowl.

Now she is on a soap opera. He's heard. He can watch her every day at noon if he chooses to. He's heard that she has a small but recurring role and that her character has some kind of ill-defined drug problem. He's heard she looks prettier on TV. He chooses not to watch. The whole town watches him not watch.

❧

He runs.

Parts of the town that border the woods are pitch-black at night. You can look into those woods and see nothing, an inky pool of endless black. The drop-off point. The end of the world. Sticks and gravel crunch beneath his feet. Once in those woods he found a doll with blood on its mouth hanging from a tree by a noose. Kids. *Boys.* A mere flirtation with evil. Still, the thought makes him run a little faster. It is two miles to the high school where he used to run cross-country, where he now circles the track in eerie night light, ghosts everywhere as always, and it is two miles back into the town.

He takes a turn onto Main Street. Everywhere there are reminders and now it is Faith's parents' house. Lately he has begun to remember, though dimly, something of the house's former owners, before the fire, something of a time before the Bannings bought and remodeled it, something of a time before, in his mind, there were flames, then ashes and rubble from which *she* emerged.

At least he is not the village idiot, he thinks, passing Derreck Wells on Main Street. He had played with Derreck Wells every day in fifth and sixth grade. In junior high they walked to school together in the next town over, day in, day out. But Derreck Wells had some kind of psychotic break in high school and is now the village idiot, a bulging-eyed crazy man who enters people's unlocked houses and stands in their living rooms.

"Hey," he says to Derreck Wells. Derreck is standing beneath a streetlight drinking beer. He is also the town drunk, begging embarrassed neighbors for the beer money his own parents refuse him. Most people are afraid of Derreck Wells, the poor son of a bitch. You couldn't see the signs of what was to come. They'd played together with plastic army men every day for two years. Every day. *For two years*.

"Hey, man, got any money?" His eyes are bloodshot. Popping out of their sockets.

"Here, brother," Sandy says, handing Derreck the couple of bills he has stashed in his sock, money he can't really afford to be giving away. What had they talked about on the way to school?

Cat is gifted, and because she is gifted she has been given a grant by the Commonwealth of Virginia to spend the summer writing a paper on the literary topic of her choice, which she has decided will be the popular misuse of the term "Lolita."

"Nabokov doesn't mean for us to take Humbert Humbert's judgments at face value," she tells Sandy. "Lolita is a male projection. In the patriarchy men invent female sexuality to alleviate their own anxiety," she says.

"I hate when that happens," he says, frowning.

He swears he sees a hint of a smile begin to form

on her lips, and he decides it is important to make the Cat girl laugh. Yes, making Cat laugh is now his goal, the only goal that he can think of. They have made love and now he lies with her, naked on the McKibbys' double bed, the double bed of those naive and guileless McKibbys.

"Lolita is not a seductress," Cat says. "She's just a girl having sex with a man."

"Like you?" he asks. He rubs her flat white stomach. She is freckled on her long, well-muscled arms and legs, but her stomach, hidden by her serious swimmer's tank suit, remains as white as a china plate. Not like Faith, whose smooth stomach was always as berry brown as the rest of her skin in summer.

"I want to know about New York," Cat says, sitting up in bed. "I want information."

"The elevators smell like human urine," he says.

"Gross," she says. "Is that all?"

"No," he says, "they've got pigeons."

Cat rises from the McKibbys' double bed and dresses. She is not at all curvaceous, but is angular here and there, and not what he's used to. But she is natural in her nakedness, unshy and unashamed. Sandy watches as she pulls on her black bicycle shorts, the jogging bra that flattens her breasts, and her thick white socks. He likes watching her dress, always for action, for endurance, for speed. He does feel moved though, despite the armature of her athletic wear, to offer her something, advice, something worldly she can arm herself with.

"Don't lose your anger at the world," he tells her.

"You sound like some old fart," she says, tying up her running shoes.

"I don't care," he says. "Fight the power, honey."

"Honey?" she says.

He kisses her good-bye and she leaves, now that darkness has completely fallen, first, separately, so that no one passing by will suspect.

The morning is wet from the spring rain, but the sun is trying to burn through and will succeed by late morning. He thought he heard a screech owl late last night. *Otis asio*. Audubon plate no. 30. He thinks it may be nesting in the rafters of the town garage. He lets the emergency brake off of the tractor and rolls silently out of the garage so as not to disturb the nest.

Will he grow old here? Has he returned for good?

I can't love you, she said when she kicked him out. Where is your life going? You scare me, she said. And, pothead.

There is a fence to be mended on the very edge of town, on the border that separates the town from a field of corn they do not own. No one can find him here as he nails new wood onto old wood. Work. One task at a time. His savior.

He walks into the cornfield. It is not well cared for and he has no idea who owns it, but it has always been here, beckoning to be disappeared into.

He imagines Faith with her sunglasses on. And why not? She is just a mortal woman after all, who gets a headache from the sun. I'm not some goddess, she said, handing him back his poems. You don't really see who I am. It was flattering at first, she said, but now . . .

He'd wanted to paint the walls of her apartment, each one a different pastel color. But by then the walls were closing in on her. Making them pretty would not dissuade those walls of hers. Those walls knew their course.

He is lying on his back in somebody's cornfield, looking at clouds. He makes a black crow sighting. *Corvus brachyrynchos.* Audubon plate no. 4. Hardly worth noting—he is, after all, lying in a fucking cornfield.

Her body is no longer his, even to dream about. Tan in summer, soft, a birthmark like a coffee stain on her left hip. Ah, the prominence of her pubic bone. *I have always loved your pubic bone, at least since I've been aware of your pubic bone, which is since Paleolithic man first made art, drawing stags that drifted eternally across a river, on the cave walls at Lascaux.*

He feels a satisfying sense of suffering, fresh as renewal, rushing in to fill him up. It is there, and without it he'd be lost. Who would he be without it? Just a man with no ambition who knows how to operate a leaf-blowing attachment. A village idiot.

He is lying in the McKibbys' master bedroom, naked on the pale blue bedspread of their double bed, waiting for Cat. He has left the back door open and she will slip inside and join him when she is done eating dinner with her parents, who, she has told him, supervise her every forkful of food.

He thinks of Faith. At first when they made love it was like incest. It had been so long, a whole life of desiring her, of watching her rub Coppertone on her bare arms and legs, a taboo. And there was the alarming fact that his brother Carey had fucked her, taken her virginity, right here in the McKibbys' house while the McKibbys were away at the Maryland shore, and bragged about it, hatefully, until Sandy had come at him with a baseball bat, ready to bash his brother's brains in. But *he* and Faith had skipped the adolescent fumbling, which he was glad of. Your brother is a terrible lover, she'd told him. It was over in five seconds. She'd only known him, Sandy, as a man who knew what he was doing. How strange to hold her actual face in his hands.

After all that time. Most men die before they hold their dream. His dream. And she had dreamed of spending her life with *him*. It is enough.

He hears the downstairs door open and footsteps entering the house. He doesn't move from his spot on the McKibbys' double bed. She knows he is up here, waiting, the breeze from a half-open window blowing across his naked body. His uncensored thoughts of Faith have given him an erection that he will rudely use to make love to another woman, though he wonders if perhaps he wasn't aroused by some unsettling combination of the two of them.

A tall dark figure appears at the bedroom door. He gasps, a sudden intake of his own breath, startled, then scared. His erection disappears. A pair of bloodshot, crazy eyes stare at him, survey his nakedness with dumb fascination.

"Derreck," he says, softly, gently, "It's me, man, Sandy." He reaches for his clothes, slowly. "I'm taking a little nap, man. Just resting up here. But now we both have to go. It's not our house, okay?"

Sandy pulls on his jeans and T-shirt.

"I wanted to ask you about the army. You think I'm too burnt out to join the army?"

"No, man, the army'd be good for you." Sandy pulls on his work boots and ties them hurriedly. "Let's go outside and talk about it."

"I need money for beer," Derreck says. "I'm starting to shake." He holds out his hand. Instinctively, Sandy grabs hold of Derreck Wells's trembling hand to steady it. He has the skin of an old man. There are people Sandy does not know living in Derreck Wells's face. There is a large smudge of dirt on his chin.

Sandy turns Derreck Wells slowly by his bony shoulder and steers him down the stairs and out of the house, locking the door behind him, taking the key with him so Derreck won't see where he keeps it hidden in the mouth of the drainpipe by the kitchen window. He ushers the shuffling Derreck Wells down Main Street to his parents' house, slowly, getting him there bit by bit.

"Did you see any action? In the war?" asks Derreck.

"No, man, I was in Germany, in peacetime, jacking off."

Derreck wants to know about the military alphabet.

Sandy tells him, "A is alpha, B is bravo, C is Charlie, D is delta, E is echo . . ."

"E is echo," says Derreck Wells, slowly, and with great effort, "I think I could learn this."

Cat speeds by on her bike, a furious, fast-moving girl. What must they look like to her, the two of them at twilight, making their way down Main Street with such labor, like old, old men. Sandy aches a moment for Derreck as he coaxes him down the street. He aches for Derreck Wells and his lost youth and potential, for youth and potential itself. For his own.

Cat shoots him a look as she whizzes by, a shrug of a look to acknowledge their failed rendezvous. Though it has only just begun, he wonders how long this can last with Cat. She will go to college. When? Next year? As soon as the fall perhaps?

"Derreck," he says, finally depositing Derreck Wells on his own front steps, "you take care of yourself now, man." He gives Derreck a small military salute.

"You were my friend," says Derreck Wells. It seems like a moment of clarity, of pristine remembrance, clear-eyed and sane. But it passes in a flash, like a glint of sunlight through the trees.

Running is the thing to stave off the edginess, otherwise he fears he will drink hard or fuck a dangerous woman, someone diseased or knife-wielding and insane. Or worse, he will simply smother gently in a narcotic cloud of marijuana. So he runs the two miles to the high school, circles the track, and runs the two miles back into town. He runs to beat the storm, for the heavens are full of their seasonal threats of rain. Thunder rolls in. Lightning lights up the sky in a sudden flash. His legs turn to knots. His lungs ache with every step.

He kicks off into a wide-open field across the street from the Bannings' house. The rain is on its way and he turns in a few dizzying circles.

The storm breaks. The rain pours. And there is no more lightning in the sky.

He slows and stops to catch his breath after the sprint. He looks up at Faith's bedroom window, which is surrounded by the hemlock trees she used to climb down, sneaking out at night to meet his brother, or his brother's best friend, or even Derreck Wells before the psychotic break.

Now, looking up at her bedroom window, where he has found himself so many times before, he waits for a vision, an hallucination of something up there. A figure. Someone dancing. A girl with her long arms outstretched, spinning, spinning. A knowledge that he can still conjure her.

Lightning strikes nearby. The air sizzles. A tree across the park is singed. Lightning really does strike people, doesn't it? He is standing in an open field waiting for a ghost while lightning strikes close enough to smell. He is going crazy like Derreck Wells. He is in danger of going crazy like Derreck Wells.

He flees, running straight for Cat, running straight to her house where he is sure she is in her bedroom, reading Nabokov's letters and *The Annotated Lolita* beneath her covers. She is in there, he is sure. She is gifted, a gift. Not a ghost. Not a figment. Cat.

Of course he cannot go inside. But he watches the rain drench the geraniums her mother has planted in clay pots near the porch, and he is reassured enough to keep from weeping.

In the light of morning shameful memories dissipate or become clouds, harmless, fluffy, and good-natured.

He drives down Main Street in the brilliant light of day to face the Banning house and its wraparound porch. Faith stood there on that porch as a five-year-old girl and asked him to punch her in the stomach. She wanted to feel what it was like to be punched in the stomach. He didn't want to do it, to hit a girl, but she begged and it was not in him to refuse her anything, even then. The blow stunned them both, and then she went running for her mother, wailing, *Sandy punched me*. He was banished and in trouble. Hitting a girl. Perhaps that is where it all began.

It is a Sunday in May and some of the old gang who still live nearby assemble in the park for a muddy game of tackle football. The pickup teams need filling out and sullen teenagers whose hell on earth it is to be trapped in uncool, quaint surroundings—not a mall in sight—have been persuaded to join it. Even Derreck Wells ambles out of his parents' house, crosses Main Street, and plops down in the muddy grass to watch. Sandy, too, has been coaxed into joining the game, and as he breathes hard, inhaling the wet earth, he is pleased by the smell of spring mud, which is caked on his elbows and his knees.

He goes out long, fumbles, and swears loudly. He bends forward to catch his breath and looks up to see, here, in broad daylight, an unexpected figure coming toward him. It is Faith coming across the park with her towheaded little niece, her sister's child, who is dressed for church in white patent leather shoes. Faith waves and encourages the little girl to wave. Sandy cannot recall the little girl's name. Or his own. Or anything else at all.

"Hey," some of the guys say.

"Hi," she says, looking right at him. She is wearing sunglasses. Why could he not be spared the sunglasses, the black sweater and the cowboy boots, spared the walk, the look, the fingernails painted red, spared the celebrity of it all; spared the greeting, the long, drawn-out, Hiii?

Hi? That is it? He'd given her his poetry. He'd

jerked off his whole life thinking of her. Now he could be anybody.

He burns, feeling his face aflame with emotions too many to comprehend. Lust, regret, hate. His heart thuds madly in his ears. Is she looking at him? Is he expected to say something? Is she speaking? Is he deaf? He nods an awkward greeting and backs away from her, tossing the football to one of the younger members of the pickup team, a boy to whom Faith Banning means nothing at all.

He fully expects that the next time he sees Faith she will be in some picturesque part of town being earnestly interviewed by the documentary film crew. How they will love one another. How they will gravitate toward one another for warmth, for life itself. How they will make each other glow. But that is not what happens. Faith startles him, peering around the garage door, her head backlit by the early morning sun. She has sought him out, intruded, and brought with her too much light for his eyes. He has the eyes of a hostage, a prisoner, he thinks.

"What are you doing down here?" he says. He is sitting on a pile of milk crates drinking coffee from a Thermos.

"I thought you might be down here," she says, taking one cautious step inside the garage door and removing her sunglasses. He looks into her face and feels, disconcertingly, as though he is looking into a mirror somehow.

"Shhh," he tells her, pointing to the rafters, "there is an owl's nest in here."

"With baby owls?" she asks.

"Not yet," he says. He screws the lid back on his Thermos.

"I'm getting married," she whispers. "I wanted to tell you that."

He looks at her, trying to absorb the information. He has been expecting some kind of news like this. He has felt it gathering, rustling in the trees. It has been coming, announcing itself on the screech of the owl, and now that it is here before him, he feels a strange kind of relief.

"The wedding will be here in the town, in the little park," she says.

"I repaired the gazebo," he finds himself telling her. "I've replaced all of the original floorboards."

"It looks beautiful," she says. "Will you come?" she asks.

He does not know what to say to the real Faith Banning who stands before him in the flesh, perhaps he never has. He sees tiny lines around her eyes that did not used to be there, tiny lines that are not visible on her TV show where she is painted for war and kindly lit. (Okay, so he watched. Once.) But the strong morning light is merciless, and her face, naked and pale and more than two years older, will not cooperate with his memory. She lives, she breathes, she marries. She will not stand frozen like a statue where he left her.

"I hope you'll consider coming," she says, slipping her sunglasses on. "He's a nice guy." She says his name. James. "Good luck," she says, backing out of the town garage, "I mean that."

Good luck. He means to turn his wit upon those words, to let them tumble around in his brain, losing meaning with every turn until he has mocked them to death and pummeled them into nothing. But Faith leaves and strangely her words rest rather peacefully in the atmosphere. He stares at the garage's threshold where she stood moments ago and wonders only when the owl's eggs will hatch. That is what he thinks of, all he wonders about.

Together he and Cat climb the stairs to the McKibbys' bedroom. He waits for her now in the kitchen, since the incident with Derreck Wells.

They take a shower together in the bathroom off of

the master bedroom, and then lie naked and damp on the blue bedspread. He has grown to love the way her collarbone juts out.

"I locked the door," he says. "Maybe we can keep Derreck from materializing on us, like the sneaky doppelgänger he is."

"They should have the film crew interview Derreck Wells," she says. "A day in the life of Derreck Wells." A joke at Derreck's expense, but not unfunny, he thinks, not unlike the remarks his brother and his friends used to make as they all tried to comprehend Derreck Wells, their old friend, one of them, now the village idiot, now another of the town's anachronisms in this, the age of enlightenment and psychopharmacology.

"Now there is the seedy underbelly for you," she says. "So why don't they take their grant money and go film that?"

"Your subversive ideas always arouse me so," he says, kissing her ear. She has three earring holes in her left ear. Three pale silver earrings.

"Are you going to tell me to fight the power now?"

"No," he says, "are you going to tell me how we live in a fascist state? Because if you are, I don't mind a bit."

"As a matter of fact, I'm not. Are you going to give me more excruciating details about birds?"

"Oh, yes," he says. He enjoys his role as boring bird enthusiast. "You know," he says, propping himself up on his elbow, "geese aren't migrating much anymore. They say that the actual longitudinal distance of migration is shortening."

"Why?" she asks, rolling her couldn't-care-less eyes elaborately. He longs to tickle her, but to tickle is to cheat.

"For reasons as yet unknown," he says. He loves her dark serious eyebrows.

"What exactly is a doppelgänger?" she says, propping herself up too. Curious, serious girl.

He pauses to recall for her the exact definition. In Germany he became a collector of foreign words for which the English language has no equivalent, like *zeitgeist* and *weltschmerz*. *Poltergeist?*

"Well?" she says impatiently.

"Since you ask," he tells her, "a doppelgänger is a ghostly double that haunts its fleshly counterpart."

Cat smirks and says, "I hate when that happens."

He watches her eyes search his face to see if he has gotten his own joke. She laughs. He had inadvertently caused her to laugh, and her laughter flutters against him, reminding him of a kiss on the eyelid.

"Get it?" she says. "Get it?"

He closes his eyes and reaches inside himself for Faith. But she will not rush in as she has always done.

She cannot be conjured to fill the vastness inside him, the endless black of the woods at night. He is just there inside it, alone and terrified with not one poem running through his mind. He is released and he knows it.

Come back. Who will he be without his broken heart?

He opens his eyes to Cat, her face there before him expected and unexpected. *There,* as present and real as the work he does each day. He clasps her hand, which he holds for a long time, while night begins to fall outside the McKibbys' house. He thinks of the dogwood trees he must plant tomorrow. And there is the porch of the Women's Club to repair because it is late spring now and nearly time for their annual rummage sale.

And everywhere there are more dead branches to clear away.